WHEN DREAMS THERE BE

ALSO BY BARBARA HINSKE

Available at Amazon in Print, Audio, and for Kindle

The Rosemont Series

Coming to Rosemont

Weaving the Strands

Uncovering Secrets

Drawing Close

Bringing Them Home

Shelving Doubts

Restoring What Was Lost

No Matter How Far

When Dreams There Be

Novellas

The Night Train

The Christmas Club (adapted

for The Hallmark Channel, 2019)

Paws & Pastries

Sweets & Treats

Snowflakes, Cupcakes & Kittens (coming 2023)

Workout Wishes & Valentine Kisses

Wishes of Home

Novels in the Guiding Emily Series

Guiding Emily

The Unexpected Path

Over Every Hurdle

Down the Aisle

Novels in the "Who's There?!" Collection

Deadly Parcel

Final Circuit

CONNECT WITH BARBARA HINSKE ONLINE

Sign up for her newsletter at **BarbaraHinske.com**
    Goodreads.com/BarbaraHinske
    Facebook.com/BHinske
    Instagram/barbarahinskeauthor
    TikTok.com/BarbaraHinske
    Pinterest.com/BarbaraHinske
    Twitter.com/BarbaraHinske
    Search for **Barbara Hinske on YouTube**
    bhinske@gmail.com

WHEN DREAMS THERE BE

THE NINTH NOVEL IN THE ROSEMONT SERIES

BARBARA HINSKE

CASA DEL NORTHERN PUBLISHING

ISBN: 978-1-7349249-92

Library of Congress Control Number: 2023905459

Casa del Northern Publishing

Phoenix, Arizona

To my remarkable husband, Brian Willis. You are the most supportive, encouraging partner in my author journey and in life itself. You make everyday a joy and an adventure.

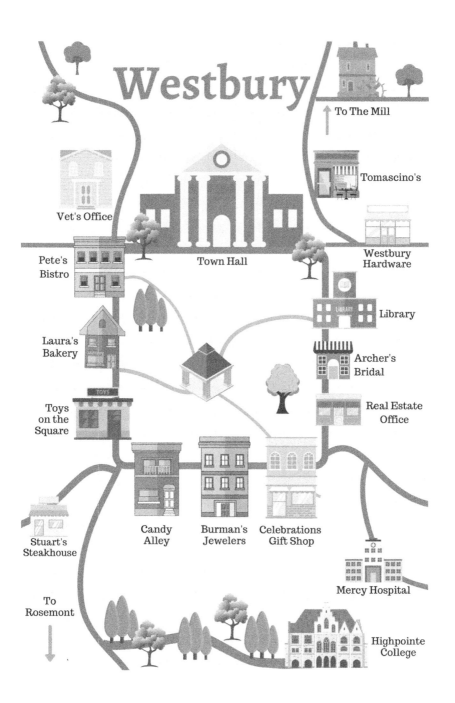

CHAPTER 1

"*D*rive... around... to..." Loretta Haynes's words were cut off by her strangled scream.

"To the maternity entrance." David finished her sentence as he turned into the main entrance of Mercy Hospital. "There are signs directing me. We'll be there in a second." He glanced nervously over his shoulder at the woman in labor in his back seat.

Dodger, his faithful companion and trained therapy dog, sat calmly next to Loretta. He turned his soulful brown eyes to meet David's, as if to affirm that it was good they'd be at the delivery room soon.

Loretta sank against the seat back and panted. "Don't park—take me right to the door."

David nodded vigorously and brought his attention back to the road. He put on his left turn signal and pulled onto a circular driveway that took him to a double set of automatic glass doors. The sign above the doors read "Delivery Drop-Off."

He put the car into park and leapt out of the door almost before the car stopped moving. David was halfway to the rear passenger door when one set of double doors opened and a man in green scrubs approached the car, pushing a wheelchair.

"Will you need one of these?" he asked.

David nodded. "I think the babies are about to come out." He opened Loretta's door as she emitted another scream.

The man reached in and put his arm around Loretta's shoulders. He helped her slide from the car into the wheelchair. "How close are the contractions?"

Loretta opened her mouth to answer, then screamed again.

The man looked at David. "How long have they been this close together?"

"The entire way here. Maybe ten minutes." David swayed nervously. "She's having twins."

The man's eyebrows shot up, and he began pushing Loretta rapidly toward the entrance. "Go park and come inside," he called over his shoulder. "You can give the admitting clerk her information. We'll take a quick look, but I think she'll be headed directly to the delivery room."

David watched until the doors closed behind Loretta's wheelchair before he got into the car again. He patted the seat next to him and Dodger lunged across the center console to take his usual seat next to his master.

"I've got to go inside to give them information about

Loretta." David stroked the dog's silky ears. "You'll have to stay in the car. It shouldn't take long." He checked the time on his dashboard clock. "Frank will be here soon."

David put the car in gear and followed the arrows directing him to Labor and Delivery Short Term Parking. He cracked the windows before exiting the car. "Be a good boy, Dodger. I know you're not used to being left alone in the car."

Dodger thumped his tail on the seat.

"I'll be back as soon as I can. You're going to be fine." David strode away from the car. He was halfway to his destination when he heard Dodger emit one sharp, quick bark. He ignored his dog and continued walking.

David entered through the glass doors that Loretta had, finding himself immersed in the typical chaos of a busy hospital maternity department. Men and women in scrubs crisscrossed in front of him, intent on their tasks. The waiting room on his left was filled with family members of all ages. He glanced to his right and found a row of desks with employees seated behind plexiglass shields. A sign above the desks read "Admitting Department. Please take a number."

David pulled a piece of paper from the machine and was looking for a place to sit when he heard his number being called on the overhead address system. He breathed a sigh of relief and went to the only open window in the Admitting Department.

The woman didn't look up at him as he sat down opposite her, on the other side of the shield. "What's your wife's name?"

"OH! No! It's not my wife."

The woman tore her eyes from her computer screen to look at him.

"It's my... she's my boss's wife. He wasn't home when she went into labor."

"Name?"

"David Wheeler."

The woman rolled her eyes. "The name of the woman who's in labor?"

Crimson spread from David's collar to the tips of his ears at his mistake. "Loretta Haynes."

"Date of birth?"

"I don't know."

The woman's hands were still, poised above her keyboard. "Address. Hers—not yours."

He gave the appropriate reply.

"Insurance?"

David shrugged. "I'm sure they have it, but I don't know anything about it."

"Does she have her purse with her?"

David shook his head. "I didn't know to grab it when I locked up the house. Her husband should be here any minute. He'll have all of that."

"If there's nothing else you can tell me, you should sit with her in the waiting room. Someone will be with you shortly."

"She's not there. They've already taken her back. Loretta's contractions weren't even a minute apart when we got here."

The woman removed her reading glasses and looked at him closely. "Are you that young man who visits here with his therapy dog?"

"I am."

"Everyone around here loves you and…"

"Dodger."

"Yes. That's the one. Thank you for doing that. You bring comfort to a lot of people in scary situations."

"We love our therapy work." David leaned toward the woman. "She's going to be all right, isn't she? She was screaming like her body was being ripped apart."

The woman's expression grew soft. "Of course she is. There's nothing unusual about that. We see it all day long. Don't worry."

"It's just that she's having twins."

"The staff here will take good care of her."

David was pushing back his chair to stand when he heard his name being called. He turned to see Frank Haynes striding toward him, with Marissa, Sean, and Nicole trailing behind.

"Where is she?" Frank asked.

The woman behind the window tapped on her keyboard and consulted her computer screen. "You're Loretta Haynes's husband?"

Frank nodded.

"They've just put her in a delivery room. Would you like to be with her?"

"Yes!"

"I'll have a nurse get you outfitted. Do you have your insurance card?"

Frank shoved his hand in his pocket and withdrew his wallet.

A nurse came up to the woman, and they exchanged a few words.

"Give your card to this young man," the woman said. "He can finish the paperwork. The nurse will take you back."

David took Frank's wallet from his shaking hand. "I'll handle the rest of this admission stuff and stay with the kids," David said, gesturing toward Loretta's children. "Don't worry, Frank."

Frank addressed his stepchildren. "Everything's going to be fine. I'll come out with news as soon as I can. David will be with you. If you need anything, ask him." He turned to the nurse, who was gesturing to him to follow her. The two set off into the interior of the hospital at a brisk pace.

CHAPTER 2

rank matched the nurse's long strides as they headed toward the delivery room. They were at the door when Frank heard a familiar voice moaning in pain. He stepped in front of the nurse and flung the door open.

The intense overhead lights ricocheted off the tile floor and white walls. Frank stopped short and put his hand up to shield his eyes. Loretta lay propped up in a bed, still and panting, amid a sea of activity. At least a dozen people, in scrubs and masks, moved swiftly around the room with orchestrated precision.

The nurse put her hand on Frank's back and urged him further into the room. "You can go to the bedside."

Frank turned to the nurse, his eyes wide. "Why are there so many people here?"

"Each child has their own team. It's routine protocol. Double the babies; double the fun. Nothing to worry about."

Frank nodded and moved to the head of Loretta's bed.

She reached for him, and he took her hand in his. "Hi, honey. Looks like—"

"I WANT TO PUSH, Frank." She cut him off. "TELL THEM I WANT TO PUSH!"

Frank, who was bending over to plant a kiss on her forehead, thought better of it and straightened.

A woman sitting on a rolling stool at the end of the bed introduced herself as the attending physician.

"I thought we were going to have a C-section," Frank said.

Loretta screamed as another contraction seized her body.

"And an epidural," Frank added.

"That may have been the plan, but there's no time for one now. Your wife was too far along by the time she got here." The doctor pointed to two sets of monitors at the bedside. "The babies are both doing well and, fortunately, the one closest to the birth canal has her head down. She can deliver this one naturally. The boy is in the breech position. I'll try to move him so his head is down after the first baby is born."

Frank hoped Loretta couldn't feel that his hand shook with fear. "What if you can't move him?"

"We'll deliver him breech or perform a C-section." She took her eyes from the monitor to look at Frank. "Don't worry. All of this is very routine. Your babies—and your wife—are going to be fine." The doctor looked at the group swirling around her before addressing Loretta. "I want you to push at the next contraction."

A nurse placed an arm under Loretta's shoulders from

her right side and told Frank to do the same from her left. When Loretta groaned with the next contraction, they lifted her shoulders. "Tuck your chin into your chest and push!" the nurse directed.

Loretta bore down.

"Good," the doctor called. "Almost there. Ease off until the next contraction."

Loretta took a shuddering breath.

Frank smoothed her hair away from her sweaty forehead. "You're doing great, honey. This is the bravest thing..."

"OWWWW..."

"Push," cried the doctor.

Frank and the nurse lifted her shoulders again, Loretta tucked her chin, and Bonnie Haynes entered the world.

The doctor handed the baby to the waiting arms of her medical team. A healthy wail soon pierced the air.

Frank laid Loretta gently against her pillow and kissed the top of her head.

"Go see her, Frank," Loretta whispered, her voice hoarse from screaming. "Tell me she's okay."

Frank nodded and started around the side of the bed. A nurse from Bonnie's team intercepted him. "We'll bring her to you in just a minute. I'm sorry we didn't ask if you wanted to cut the umbilical cord."

"That's okay... I'm fine with you doing it," Frank replied quickly.

"Her Apgar score is great," the nurse said. "And she's a whopping six pounds seven ounces. That's huge for a twin."

She turned as another nurse brought the crying baby to them and showed Bonnie to her parents.

"Can I hold her?" Loretta said, reaching up to touch Bonnie's cheek.

The doctor, still positioned at the end of the bed, spoke up. "Let's have Dad hold her first. You still have another baby to deliver."

The nurse held the whimpering bundle out to Frank. He took a step back. "That's a newborn. I don't know how to…"

The nurse laughed. "You're about to become an expert at handling a newborn. Your daughter is strong and healthy. She won't break." The nurse placed Bonnie into Frank's reluctant arms.

He cradled her against his chest. Their eyes met and Bonnie stopped fussing. Frank felt his knees buckle and took a step to regain his balance. He recalled the scene in *The Grinch Who Stole Christmas*, where the Grinch's heart grew three sizes. Frank now knew what that felt like. His gaze swept the face of the tiny person who—along with her brother—would change the lens through which he would view the world from this day forward.

"I'm going to turn your other baby," the doctor said. "You may feel some pressure."

Loretta gasped and grabbed the mattress on either side of her. She squeezed her eyes shut.

Frank swung his gaze to the doctor.

Her expression turned from one of serious concentration into a satisfied smile. "There. That son of yours was very cooperative. He's now head down and ready to join his sister."

"I'm too tired," Loretta said. "I can't push anymore."

"Can you do just one more?" the doctor asked.

Loretta looked at Frank.

He shifted Bonnie to one arm and grasped Loretta's hand. She nodded.

A contraction came, and another nurse raised Loretta's shoulders while she pushed with every remaining ounce of strength.

Branson Haynes was delivered into the doctor's waiting hands. The second medical team took charge of him and soon the air was filled with the most joyful sound in a delivery room—the healthy wail of not one, but two newborns.

CHAPTER 3

*F*rank hurried to find the other children as soon as they'd settled Loretta into her room and had taken the babies to the nursery for additional examination. Loretta had assured him she and the babies were fine. He needed to give the kids the good news.

He checked a clock on the wall as he walked down a long hallway and was shocked to see that it was almost nine o'clock. Time had gone at warp speed since he'd walked into the hospital in the middle of the afternoon. The kids would be hungry and exhausted—and probably anxious and scared —waiting for news.

He rounded the corner and stepped into the crowded waiting area. The scene at the far end of the room reignited his already-raw emotions. Susan Scanlon sat in a molded plastic chair between Sean and Marissa, with Nicole on her lap. The older two children were peacefully reading books. Nicole was asleep. David was nowhere to be seen.

Frank swept his hand across his eyes and blinked hard before crossing the room to them.

Marissa was the first to see him approaching. "Dad!" She leapt out of her chair, tossing her book on her seat, and ran to him.

Sean was on her heels. "Is Mom okay?"

"Your mother is great. And so are your little brother and sister."

Nicole stirred at the sound of her father's voice.

"Your daddy's here with great news," Susan murmured to Nicole as she slid the little girl off her lap. The two of them stood as Frank, Marissa, and Sean joined them.

"Bonnie and Branson were born about two hours ago. They're both healthy and have been crying up a storm."

"That's not good if they're crying, is it?" Sean asked.

"Actually—it's exactly what newborns are supposed to do. It means their lungs are fully developed. They both have full heads of dark hair. They're… they're perfect. And your mother is the most remarkable woman in the world," he said. "Giving birth to twins is a lot of work, but she was the bravest person ever. They just moved her to her room and have taken Bonnie and Branson to the nursery."

"Can we go see them?" Marissa asked.

"Not tonight. Your mom needs to rest and so do the babies."

"No… I want to see Mom," Nicole whined.

"It's okay, honey. You'll see her—and the twins—tomorrow. Hospitals do important work and have rules they have to follow," Susan interjected.

"I'm sorry you've been waiting so long," Frank said. "I'll bet you're hungry. Let me go back to say goodbye to your mother and I'll take you home. We'll pick up food on the way."

"You'll stay right here, Frank," Susan said. "I'll take the kids back to your place and spend the night with them there. And I'll get these guys off to school in the morning."

"Are you sure? That's a lot to ask on short notice."

"It's no problem. I am Nicole's half-sister, after all. Aaron isn't on call tonight, so he's got Julia. I had a trial scheduled to start tomorrow, but the matter settled last Thursday, so I've got a lot of free time this week. If you need me to bring the kids to the hospital after school, I can do that, too."

Frank marveled, as he often did, at the warmth and kindness of his newly found friends in Westbury. "That may not be necessary. If Loretta and the babies continue to do this well, they'll all be going home tomorrow."

"Wow! I thought they'd keep her an extra day since she had a C-section."

"Actually, she didn't. They came too fast."

"My goodness. And the babies are big enough to come home right away?"

"Yes. They were both over six pounds."

Susan took an involuntary step back. "All I can say is... ouch!"

"That wife of mine is incredible."

"She certainly is. Give me a heads-up when you know if

you'll be coming home tomorrow. We've got a casserole brigade ready to swing into action."

"What's that?"

"All your friends have signed up to bring you dinner for the next three weeks."

"That's so nice."

"It's what friends do for new parents."

"Speaking of food," Frank reached for his wallet, "you must be starved."

"We ate dinner in the cafeteria," Susan said. "Marissa called me right after you got here. I packed a bag and came over."

"And I told David about the key we hide in that fake rock by the back door," Sean said. "When Susan got here, he went to our house to feed and walk Snowball, Sally, and Daisy."

"You've thought of everything." Frank smiled at his family. "That's very grown up of you. I'm impressed."

Nicole yawned.

Frank opened his arms to the stepchildren he loved and swept them into a group hug. "Be good for Susan and don't worry about a thing. You'll see your mother and your new siblings tomorrow."

"Does Loretta have her hospital bag?" Susan caught Frank's gaze over the tops of the children's heads. "I forgot to ask David if they brought it."

Frank stared back with a deer-in-the-headlights look. He shrugged.

Susan smiled. "I'll look when we get home. If it's still there, I'll drop it off here after I take the kids to school. Do you have clothes to take the babies home from the hospital in? Are the car seats installed in one of your cars?"

Frank shook his head continuously as she talked. "I guess we weren't prepared—yet."

"No worries. I'll call my mom and we'll get you sorted." She reached over and patted his elbow. "You look like you could use some rest yourself. They'll let you spend the night in the room with Loretta."

"That's what they said. I figured I'd need to go home. I'm glad I can stay." He straightened, and Sean and Marissa retrieved their books.

"One last piece of advice—that was given to me and that I, sadly, ignored. Let the hospital keep the babies in the nursery so the two of you can get as much rest as possible. You'll have them full time soon enough. This may be your last chance for an uninterrupted night's sleep for a very long time."

CHAPTER 4

rank checked the time on his cell phone, shielding the screen with his hand so the light wouldn't wake Loretta. He'd been stretched out in the recliner next to her hospital bed, listening to her faint snores for hours. Based on what she'd been through, she deserved to sleep.

He was also exhausted, but his mind replayed the births of his children—*his children*—over and over, as if on a replay loop. No matter how hard he tried, he couldn't quiet his mind.

Frank shifted his weight, slowly pressing his feet to the floor to lower the footrest on the recliner. The chair closed itself with a thwack. He swung his gaze to Loretta and held his breath.

She didn't stir.

Frank stood and tiptoed to the door. He opened it just

wide enough to slip into the hallway, and pulled it shut behind him without making a sound.

The hallway lights were dim. The nurse's station, positioned in the center of a pod of rooms that circled it, was a hubbub of activity.

Frank approached the counter. He didn't recognize any of the nurses. He caught the eye of one of them and asked where he could see his babies.

The woman directed him to the nursery, at the other end of the hall, past the elevators.

Frank made his way to the long glass window. Hospital bassinets lined the window on the other side. He moved from bassinet to bassinet, searching for Bonnie and Branson. He didn't find them. A frisson of alarm ran down his spine. He went back to the beginning and retraced his steps, focusing intently on each face. His children were not there.

He stepped to the door of the nursery. A sign read "No admittance. Medical Personnel Only." He tried the door. It was locked.

A nurse passed by and he knocked on the glass. She turned to him and came to the door.

"My babies," he said, the anguish in his voice audible through the glass barrier. "They're not here."

The nurse opened the door a crack. "You are?"

He gave his name and the names of the twins.

The woman nodded and opened the door wide for him to enter. "Your babies are fine," she said. "Twins are always considered high risk, so we've got them closer to the nurse's station. Would you like to see them?"

Frank nodded vigorously.

"We've got a visiting room right over here." She pointed to a small, windowless room to her left. "Go on in and I'll bring them to you."

"Thank you so much. When I didn't see them... I just..."

The nurse patted his arm. "I'll be right back."

She returned, rolling one bassinet containing two babies, nestled against each other. They were both sleeping.

Frank released a slow breath.

"They're both so big, we almost couldn't get them into the same bassinet."

"Should we keep them together at home? We bought two cribs."

"There's no right or wrong, but I'd separate them. I had twins, and it was so much easier to get them settled down when they were in their own cribs." She glanced at the babies. "They look angelic now, but wait until they're both crying. You'll want to do everything you can to prevent one of them from waking the other."

"Good to know. Thank you." Frank hovered over the top of the bassinet, staring in wonder at the two people who now meant everything to him.

"I'll leave you to visit on your own. I'll come back to check on you in twenty minutes, but you can press this button"—she pointed to a call button on the wall—"if you need anything."

Frank nodded but kept his eyes riveted on his children. "Hey," he whispered, "I'm your dad. Your mom's asleep.

Giving birth to you was really hard on her, so we have to let her rest."

He was mesmerized by the gentle rise and fall of their chests. They were breathing in unison.

"Your mom is the kindest, bravest, and most admirable person I've ever met. I married way above my pay grade with her. I'm still not sure how I got so lucky." He extended his hand and touched the folds of the blanket that swaddled Branson.

"I'm not an evil man. But I've done some terrible things. Things I'm ashamed of." He choked on the next words. "I'm a… felon. You don't know what that means, but you will. You'll learn that about me, one day. Kids at school will tell you—they may even make fun of you because of the bad things I've done."

He paused and hung his head. "I hope you won't be ashamed of me for that. If I could undo the past, I would. I've completed my community service and paid my fine. People —my friends—have forgiven me. Your mother sees me as the good person I've learned to be. She's made me a better man."

The babies slept on.

Frank put his hand over his eyes. "I promise you I will live every day, for the rest of my life, being the kind of man and father that you can be proud of." His voice was thick with emotion. "I want the best possible future for you and the rest of our family."

He pulled his hand away from his eyes and looked down into the clear blue eyes of his daughter.

Bonnie shifted her weight inside her blanket. Her eyes remained open wide, fixed on his.

Frank held his breath.

When Frank remembered the incident in the years ahead, he swore Bonnie winked at him before closing her eyes and going back to sleep.

CHAPTER 5

Susan pulled into the driveway of Frank and Loretta's home after she'd dropped Sean, Marissa, and Nicole at their respective schools. She and her husband, orthopedic surgeon Aaron Scanlon, wanted a second child. This morning convinced her they should start trying. Julia would be two soon and she wanted her children to be close enough in age to be able to attend the same school at the same time. Frank and Loretta would be driving children all over town for the next decade.

Three cars were idling at the curb in front of the house, with another stopped across the street.

Susan got out of her car as Joan Torres, Gloria Harper, Nancy Knudsen, and Tonya Holmes approached her. She smiled, remembering how generous and helpful these same women had been when she'd first come home from the hospital with Julia.

"Judy Young called to say she's waiting for a delivery at Celebrations and couldn't get away. She's hoping the crib pads Loretta ordered from her weeks ago will be in the shipment. If they are, she'll stop by when she closes the store at five," Joan said.

"What's our plan?" Susan asked.

Nancy shifted a bucket filled with cleaning supplies from one arm to the other. "Tonya and I are going to give the house a good cleaning. Frank told my husband that Loretta refused to hire cleaners."

"Seriously? What was she thinking?" Susan said.

"I'll bet she'll change her mind, now that she's got two newborns," Nancy said. "Tonya and I agreed we'd get the place shipshape before she comes home."

"I like to clean," Tonya said. "Unlike my work on the Town Council, I can see instant results from my efforts when I clean."

"Gloria and I will tidy up the kitchen and make a list of the groceries we think she'll need," Joan said.

"And I threw together a lasagna for Glenn and me for our dinner tonight. If Loretta comes home this afternoon, I'll bake it and bring it to them, instead," Gloria said.

"That's nice of you—and Glenn." Susan's eyes twinkled.

"I'm not sure he knows about it," Gloria quipped, "but I'm sure he won't mind. He's grown very fond of Frank."

"I called my mom on the way over here," Susan said. "She said she'd send out an email to the group that's signed up to bring meals to the family for the next three weeks. I know all of us have included our names on the list. The first day of that rotation will start tomorrow."

Susan turned and led the band of helpful friends to the front door. "I know I've said it before." She inserted the key in the lock. "But it bears repeating. I don't know what I would have done without all of you during those early weeks when Julia had colic. I swear I would have lost my mind."

Gloria put her hand on Susan's back. "We've all been there, honey—had times where we needed help from others. It's a privilege to give back."

Susan pushed the door open and was inundated by the effusive greetings of Snowball, Sally, and Daisy. She leaned down to pat each one, speaking to them by name and admonishing them to calm down. "I'll put these guys in the backyard," she said.

The women followed her inside.

Tonya stumbled over a pair of sneakers left in the entryway. A skateboard was propped against the wall. A note reminding Frank of a soccer practice for Sean from four months earlier was taped to the mirror above a console table loaded with books, empty water bottles, and papers. "Looks like we've got our work cut out for us," Tonya said.

"Let's get crackin'," Joan said. "What are you going to do, Susan?"

"Loretta doesn't have her hospital bag with her, and they'll need clothes to bring the babies home in. I'll grab those things and take them to the hospital. The car seats also need to be installed in the SUV that Loretta usually drives, since they may be released today. I've never installed them before but I'm sure I can figure it out. I'll tackle that when I get back."

"I'll call Sam to come over and do that." Joan said.

"Really?" Susan couldn't hide her relief. "Isn't he working?"

Joan and Gloria exchanged a glance. "If you call helping Glenn restore his old mustang work, then he's working."

"I'll bet they'll both come over," Gloria said. "As I mentioned, Glenn really likes Frank and will want to help."

The women set to their tasks. The house was soon filled with congenial conversation and the satisfying smells of cleaning products.

Susan emerged from Frank and Loretta's bedroom with Loretta's packed overnight bag. "I went into the nursery and none of the baby clothes have been washed," Susan said. "Do you think I should run a load before I bring clothes for Bonnie and Branson to come home in?"

Gloria was the first to respond. "Why would you do that, dear?"

"The sizing and manufacturing chemicals on new clothing might irritate their skin. The babies could be allergic, too."

Gloria and Joan exchanged glances. "Even if that's true, they'd just be coming home from the hospital in them. We can wash everything while you're gone so they can change into freshly laundered clothes when they get home if the clothes you take—bother them." She gave Susan an encouraging smile.

Susan shook her head. "No. I don't think so. I'll go home

and pick up some of Julia's baby clothes to take to the hospital. They're all clean and packed into totes in her closet. That way we don't have to worry about it."

Joan shrugged while Gloria patted Susan's arm. "Whatever you think best."

"We'll make sure the rest of these baby clothes are washed," Joan said. "Although I've never heard of clean clothes hurting anyone," she teased.

"I'm being paranoid, aren't I?" Susan looked chagrined. "When Julie was an infant, my mom told me I read too much on the internet about things that could go wrong."

"You're just being careful," Gloria said. "Nothing wrong with that. If it makes you feel better, go home and get those clean baby clothes."

Susan pursed her lips. "I think I will. See you all when I get back. We should know by then if they're coming home today or tomorrow." She sailed out the door and the other women got back to work.

CHAPTER 6

*D*avid drove past the Haynes' home. The driveway was full of cars and the curbs on either side of the street were occupied. Frank's car wasn't among them.

He didn't want to intrude, but he was eager for news. After dropping Loretta off at the hospital, he had a vested interest in the outcome. He'd texted Frank but hadn't received a response.

David glanced at Dodger, riding shotgun as usual. "What do you think, boy? Should I go in and ask?"

Dodger thumped his tail on the seat.

David parallel parked three houses down and got out of his car. "You'll have to wait here, boy. I won't be long."

Dodger settled into the seat and rested his muzzle on his paws.

The front door opened wide as he walked up the sidewalk. Joan Torres and Gloria Harper greeted him as they hurried to Joan's car.

"Are they home yet?" he asked.

"No. They're all coming home today. We know that for sure, but we don't know when," Gloria said. "We're on the way to the grocery to get milk, bread, fruit—basic staples that they're low on."

"Then we're going to Gloria's to pick up lasagna for their dinner tonight," Joan said.

"That's all I wanted to know." David turned around and made his way to his car.

"Can I make a suggestion?" Gloria stopped walking and turned to him.

"Sure."

"Go on in and find Sean. He seems very anxious about his mother and uncomfortable with all the hubbub and strange women running around his house."

David looked over his shoulder at the house. "I'd feel the same way."

"Both girls are helping us get ready for the twins to come home and are having a blast, but Sean is like a fish out of water."

"I'm headed to Forever Friends when I leave here," David said. "I don't normally work at the shelter on Mondays, but I promised Frank I would put in extra hours when the babies were born. I'll take a minute to talk to Sean, first."

"That's a great idea," Gloria said. "He idolizes you, you know. Glenn told me."

David blushed.

"If you're here when I get back with the lasagna, I'm sure you can stay for supper. There'll be plenty," Gloria said as she and Joan continued to the car.

"Thanks," David called after them. He continued to the front door and stepped into the busy household. The vacuum was running in the back of the house. Marissa was in the dining room folding an enormous pile of laundry that sat on one end of the table.

"David." Susan rushed past with Nicole at her side.

"Is Sean here?" he asked.

"In his room. With the door closed," Nicole said.

David made his way to his young friend's room and knocked on the door.

"Yeah," came the response from inside.

"It's David. Can I come in?"

After a brief interlude, the door swung open. "I didn't know it was you," Sean said.

"What're you up to in here?" David asked.

Sean shrugged. "I finished my homework. Now I'm just playing online games."

"Why aren't you out there, helping?"

"I tried. Marissa says I don't know how to fold baby clothes." He rolled his eyes. "Like there's a right way. I took out the trash and moved the rocking chair into my mom's room, but after that there wasn't much for me to do. I kept getting in the way."

"I'm sure they're all nervous about the babies coming home." David tilted his head to one side. "If you want to help Frank, why don't you come to Forever Friends with me?"

"I'm supposed to be here when they get home with the babies."

"Will they call when they're leaving the hospital?"

Sean nodded. "Dad said he'll text when they're on their way."

"I'm stopping by to exercise the dogs and assess any new ones that were turned in over the weekend. That shouldn't take more than a couple of hours. If you come with me, the two of us can cut the time in half. And if Frank texts that they're on the way home, we'll leave right away. I can have you back here before they get home."

"You'd do that?"

"Of course. I'd appreciate the help, and I'd go crazy in your shoes. Waiting isn't easy."

"I have to get trained on all the stuff you do at Forever Friends if I'm going to fill in for you when you leave," Sean said.

"I move to California in six weeks. I'm so excited to take that job as a kennel assistant at the Guide Dog Center. We need to spend as much time together as possible before then," David agreed.

Sean searched for his shoes.

"I'll go tell... someone out there... what our plan is," David said.

Sean nodded.

"I'll meet you out front," David said.

Sean pulled his sneakers from under his bed and began stuffing his feet into them. "I can't wait to get out of here. I'll be right behind you."

DAVID SWIPED his key card at the rear entrance to Forever Friends and he, Sean, and Dodger followed the familiar path to the dog kennels. They passed a volunteer escorting an elderly woman and a long-haired dachshund puppy to the adoption desk.

"Hey, buddy." David bent down and stroked the tiny furry head. "You've found your forever home!" He looked at the woman. "He's a sweet guy. You've picked a good one."

The woman beamed. "I hope so. I knew the minute I saw him. And he's just the right size for me." She and the volunteer continued on their way.

"It's almost closing time," David said to Sean. "The night crew will feed all the dogs first, then take them out to the exercise yard in small groups to run around while they clean the kennels."

"Do you separate them by size?"

"That's part of it—and temperament. We occasionally have dogs who don't get along well with other animals. We take them out for walks by themselves."

David took them to a cabinet in the corner and opened a bottom bin. He thrust his hand into a stash of dog treats, scooping up a large handful that he stuffed into his jacket pocket. He stepped to one side. "Here—load up your pocket, as well. The key to success—especially with the dogs that come in here with behavioral issues—is to give them plenty of love and lots of treats."

Sean followed David's lead.

Dodger, who had been ambling along with them, now uttered a short bark.

David tossed him a treat and Dodger caught it in mid-air.

"I like all the dogs," David said, "but my favorite thing is working with the ones who are fearful and anxious. It's really great to help an animal get over that and find their forever home." He pointed toward the adoption area. "Like that guy. He was a mess when he came in here. We figure he must have been on the streets for weeks. His ringworm was so bad that he had almost no coat left. And he cowered from everyone."

"Did you work with him?"

"Yep. It took some time, but look at him now. I'll bet he'll spend the evening on that lady's lap and sleep next to her. There'll be no shortage of treats in that house, either."

Sean nodded. "I can see why you like doing this."

"Let's get to know the new dogs that came in over the weekend." David consulted a clipboard on the wall next to the cabinet. "There are three of them—all strays. Two lab mixes and an all-purpose mutt. We keep them separate from the other animals for three days—or five days if they have a microchip. If they came in as strays, that gives their owners time to find them."

"Do people find their lost dogs very often?"

"Sure—maybe a quarter of the dogs that come in as strays end up being returned to their owners. That's the best—seeing the dogs reunited with their people. It's pure joy, all around."

"I know how I'd feel if one of our dogs was lost and we got it back," Sean said.

"During that waiting period, we get to know the dog to figure out if they're housebroken, if they get along with other dogs, and what their general temperament is. At the end of the waiting period, we neuter them and give them a medical exam. We're committed to helping the ones who never get reunited with their owners—or never had a home in the first place. We don't want to send out a dog that has medical or emotional problems."

"You know how to do that?"

"I've learned, during my time working here."

"That's so cool."

"Frank's been a big help with all of that. So has the rest of the staff. Some of them have been here for more than twenty years."

"Wow. Do you think I can learn all this stuff?"

"Of course you can. I did."

David walked to a kennel bearing a photograph of a yellow lab mix. The card next to the photo noted it was a male, sixty-five pounds, and estimated to be three years old.

They peered into the kennel.

"Is he outside with the other big dogs?" Sean asked.

"Nope," David said. He pointed to a rug bunched up at the far corner of the kennel. The rug moved almost imperceptibly. "He's hiding under that rug."

"I didn't see him. You're right."

"This one has fear issues."

"Will he bite us?" Sean took a step back.

"We're not going to challenge him," David said. "First, we'll talk to him softly and calmly from right here. Allow him to get accustomed to our voices. Pay close attention to see if he sticks his nose in our direction or lifts his head up. When he does, we'll offer him a treat."

David began talking to the animal. "Good boy. Nice dog. You're safe now. No one is going to hurt you."

The dog shoved his nose out from under the blanket.

"There you go," David said. "Hungry? Would you like a treat?" He took a treat from his pocket and stuck his hand through the bars of the kennel, holding it out to the dog.

The nose twitched as it picked up the smell of the treat.

"Come on, boy. Do you want a treat?"

The dog inched his head out of the blanket.

David remained still, holding the treat out as far as he could reach.

The dog didn't move.

David raised the treat up and waggled it.

The dog followed it with his eyes but remained still.

David placed the treat on the floor of the cage and pulled his hand back. The dog shifted his weight under the blanket.

David and Sean held their breath.

Nothing moved.

Sean swung to David. "Now what?"

David took a handful of treats from his pocket and tossed them into the cage, close to the blanket. He and Sean stepped to the next kennel and hovered, almost out of sight, and watched.

The dog slithered out of the blanket and tentatively snatched first one and then the rest of the treats.

A grin spread across David's face.

"What do we do now?" Sean asked. "Do you try to get him to take them from your hand?"

"Not today. Did you see how his hind legs shook as he approached the treats? We may have to go through this same routine for several days before he's comfortable with us." He headed back to the clipboard. "Don't worry. We'll get him to like us. Let's see where our next dog is."

Sean's phone vibrated in the pocket of his jeans. He reached for it and read the text message. The look on his face told David everything he needed to know.

"They're on their way home, aren't they?"

Sean nodded.

David called to one of the kennel staff who was cleaning out a stall. "We've got to go. This one," he pointed to the kennel where they'd just been working, "is all done. Sorry we can't stay to help with the others."

"No worries," the worker said. "We've got this."

David sped down the hallway at a trot, with Dodger and Sean at his heels.

CHAPTER 7

"SUSAN." Marissa ran out of the dining room, clutching a stack of folded receiving blankets to her chest. She headed down the hallway toward the nursery.

Susan stepped out of Nicole's room and intercepted Marissa.

"They're on their way home! Frank just texted. He was headed to the parking garage to bring the car around."

"Does he know Sam switched out Frank's car for Loretta's—with the car seats installed?" Susan asked.

"I don't know," Marissa replied. "I sure hope so—or he'll be searching for the wrong car."

Joan overheard their conversation from the kitchen. She joined them in the hallway. "Sam told me he texted Frank to tell him the spot number in the garage where he'd parked Loretta's car and confirmed Frank had the key."

Nicole came out of her room and put her arms around Susan's waist.

"Good. That's covered. What else do we need to do before they get here?" Susan asked.

"This is the last load of laundry." Marissa held up the stack she was carrying.

"Gloria put her lasagna in the oven at 200 degrees to stay warm. She wrapped a loaf of garlic bread in foil and stuck it in there, too," Joan said. "We picked up greens, a cucumber, and tomatoes at the grocery store and threw together a salad that's now in the fridge." She turned to Marissa. "You're all set for dinner."

"Thank you," Marissa murmured.

"I think that's everything," Susan said.

Gloria met up with them, wiping her hands on a dish towel. Tonya was right behind her.

"The four of us should clear out of here," Gloria said, glancing from Susan to Joan and then Tonya. "The kitchen is tidy, and the house is clean. It's time to let this family welcome Bonnie and Branson without all of Westbury looking over their shoulders."

"I agree," Tonya said. "I'm eager to see those babies, as I'm sure we all are, but I can wait."

The other women nodded their agreement.

"We can do that when we bring dinner over on our night," Tonya said to Marissa. "I posted the meal sign-up chart on the front of your refrigerator. You've got dinners scheduled for the next three weeks. The plan is for the meal to be here by four o'clock. I've got the phone number of everyone listed on the date they signed up for, so you can call to reschedule if you need to."

"We're home from school by four. I'm sure that'll be fine," Marissa replied.

"I've arranged for my nanny to start early every day this week so I can drive all of you to school. That way, Frank and Loretta can concentrate on adjusting to having two newborns in the house," Susan said. "Will you tell your parents?"

"I'll do it," Nicole piped up.

Gloria smiled at the little girl. "It's so helpful when everyone chips in."

"I guess that's it," Susan said. "Is there anything else you need from us before we clear out of here?" She looked from Marissa to Nicole.

The girls exchanged a glance and shook their heads.

"This is a very special time." Gloria addressed both girls. "I had nine children and the older kids always loved welcoming the newest edition to our family. Your world is about to turn upside down—one newborn creates a lot of chaos, let alone two. I hope you give each other a lot of grace. If there's anything I can do—for any of you—my number's on that schedule. All you have to do is call."

"That goes for me, too," Susan said.

"Actually—make that all of us," Joan interjected. "And now we'd better get going or we'll be standing here when they pull into the driveway."

Susan hugged Nicole and Marissa and then followed the other women out to their cars.

DAVID PULLED to the curb in front of Sean's house as Joan's car receded down the street. "Looks like they've all left."

"That's good," Sean said. "It was too busy with them there." He reached for his door handle. "Will you go to Forever Friends tomorrow after school?"

David nodded. "I want to work with that stray. It's the best feeling, to help get a dog over its fear of people."

"Could I go with you?"

"Sure, if your parents say it's okay. Do you come home after school? I get out later than you do, so I can pick you up on my way."

"I think so. Mom always picked us up after school. Things might be different now…"

"You'll find out soon. Text me when you know the plan. We'll figure something out. I'd like your help."

"Okay… cool." The younger boy got out of the car and walked around the house to the backyard, a new confidence in his step.

David drove away.

Sean was coming in the back door as Frank, Loretta, and the new babies pulled into the garage.

"They're here," Nicole shouted from the living room window seat, where she'd been keeping watch.

Sally and Snowball barked and pranced at the door into the house from the garage.

"Sean," Marissa called. "Is that you?"

"Yeah," he replied, shutting the back door behind him.

"Put the dogs outside."

"You're not the boss of me."

Marissa found him opening the refrigerator door.

"Please, Sean. All three of them obey you. We don't want them jumping all over Mom and the babies."

"Okay," he said, slamming the refrigerator shut. He put two fingers between his teeth and whistled as he walked to the back door.

The three dogs met him there, and he ushered them outside. "Be good. No yipping or digging at the door, understand?" Three tails wagged in unison. "I'll feed you as soon as I meet my new brother and sister."

He joined his siblings at the door to the garage.

"What's taking them so long?" Nicole asked.

"They have to get them out of car seats," Marissa said. "If they're asleep, they won't want to wake them."

Nicole opened the door.

A plaintive wail emanated from one of the babies. The other joined in.

Frank appeared from one side of the car and Loretta from the other. They each held a baby, crying at full force.

"Oh, boy," Sean muttered.

Marissa swiveled her head over her shoulder to give him a stern glance, then turned back to Frank and Loretta.

"Welcome home!" Nicole cried.

Loretta smiled at her older children, waiting anxiously in the open doorway. She moved gingerly.

"You okay, Mom?" Sean asked in alarm.

"I'm fine," Loretta answered. "Just a bit sore—which is

normal." She raised her voice to be heard above the crying baby in her arms and stepped inside. "This," she said, turning sideways and lowering one arm so they got a good view of the red face, "is your brother, Branson."

Branson paused, and as if on cue, opened his eyes. He took one look at his older brother and sisters, and resumed crying.

"And this is Bonnie," Frank said, a slight tone of panic in his voice.

Marissa, Sean, and Nicole stepped close, examining their new siblings.

"What do you do with them now?" Sean asked.

"I'd planned to have this talk before these guys arrived, but... well... we all know that didn't happen," Loretta said. "Anyway—I'll need help from all of you. I've decided to breastfeed them, and to make that workable, we'll have to get them on the same schedule. That means we're going to put up with crying if one of them is hungry between feedings."

Sean's eyes grew big. "It sounds like something's wrong with them."

"They're fine. They were both over six pounds, so waiting a few minutes to be fed won't hurt them."

Bonnie and Branson continued to wail.

Frank shifted his weight from foot to foot.

The sound of barking from the backyard added to the cacophony.

"What do you need us to do?" Marissa asked.

"You can burp them after they've been fed. And rock them back to sleep."

"I can change diapers," Marissa said. "I learned how when I babysat Julia."

"That would be incredibly helpful."

"I'll play with them," Sean said. "Show them stuff."

Loretta ruffled his hair. "That'll be great when they're older. Newborns eat and sleep—that's about it. Their care is going to consume most of our time," she said, glancing at Frank, "but we're still your parents and we're here for you, too. I want you to tell me about your days and everything we've always shared."

"That's right," Frank said. "I know I get busy at work, but I want you to come to me at any time. Don't feel you're interrupting. Your mother is still recovering from giving birth, and feeding these guys every two or three hours will be exhausting, so we need to let her get as much rest as possible." Frank took Loretta's arm and urged her toward their bedroom.

"There's nothing for me to do to help," Nicole said in a small voice.

Loretta swung to face her. "There's a big thing you can do. Will you make sure I always have a full bottle of water nearby? Nursing moms need to drink lots of water. That's very important."

Nicole nodded solemnly.

"Great," Loretta said. "We'll get into the swing of things before you know it. I'm going to nurse these two now. Then you can hold them and rock them if you want to. They'll be happier once they're fed."

"Are you hungry?" Frank asked the kids. "You can order a pizza."

"Gloria left a lasagna in the oven," Marissa said.

"And salad and bread," Nicole added.

"That sounds lovely," Loretta said. "I'll feed the twins and then we'll all settle in for a nice dinner. You can catch me up on everything I've missed."

Frank cast an admiring glance at his wife. She evidently hadn't experienced the terror he had at the hospital, when at least one of the babies had either been crying or nursing. Their demands had been unending, and he couldn't imagine how they would cope at home.

"Frank and I will take the babies into our room to nurse. I'm still working out the best positions to do this."

"Nicole and I will set the table," Marissa said.

"And I'll feed the dogs," Sean chimed in.

Loretta smiled at her capable children and headed down the hallway.

FRANK CHECKED the time on his phone as he plugged it into the charger on his nightstand. It was only 11:30. He routinely stayed up past midnight, but it now felt like it was the middle of the night. He rubbed his hand across his stubble and carefully crawled into bed next to Loretta.

They'd fed the babies for the third time since they'd been home. He'd changed and swaddled Branson—the last to finish—and both babies were sleeping in bassinets at the foot of the bed.

He rolled onto his side to watch Loretta's face in the swath of moonlight that fell across the bed from a break in the curtains. He marveled at everything they'd been through —everything she'd given him.

Loretta stirred and rolled away from him.

He inched closer and drew her to him, holding her reverently. They'd habitually fallen asleep like spoons until the weight of the babies had made that sleeping position uncomfortable for her. He yearned for it.

Frank sighed with contentment, shut his eyes, and drifted off to sleep.

Bonnie's distinctive cry was the first to wake them, followed closely by Branson's.

Loretta was already on her feet when he threw the covers back and got out of bed. He caught sight of the bedside clock. It was only 1:30. They hadn't even gotten two hours of sleep. He moaned inwardly.

Frank looked at his wife, bending over Bonnie's bassinet. His heart surged. He should be ashamed of himself. To be woken by his own child was a problem he'd longed for and given up hope of ever experiencing.

Frank picked up Branson with a grateful heart.

CHAPTER 8

"They're here." Maggie Martin stopped rinsing breakfast dishes and wiped her hands on her apron.

John Allen set his coffee cup on the counter and went to the front door of Rosemont. He swung the heavy mahogany door open wide.

Maggie joined him at the top of the steps leading to the impressive entryway. They put their arms around each other's waists and watched as Aaron pulled to a stop.

Susan leapt out of the passenger seat and opened the rear door to unstrap Julia from her car seat.

The little girl raced to meet Maggie as she came down the steps to sweep her granddaughter into a hug. Julia accepted a hug and kiss, then wriggled free of Maggie's embrace to throw herself at John.

John and his first wife had never had children. Julia had

been his first close relationship with an infant, and he was completely smitten. The entire town knew he was wrapped around her little finger and teased him about spoiling her. John didn't care. Julia was the best thing that had ever happened to him—after meeting and marrying Maggie Martin—and he didn't care who knew it.

Maggie shook her head as she grinned at John. "I guess we know who her favorite is."

"Don't feel bad, Mom," Susan said, joining her. "We think she prefers John to both of us." She pointed to herself and then to Aaron.

Maggie chuckled. "So, what're the two of you going to do this weekend while we keep Julia? Any big plans or are you lying low?"

"A bit of both, we hope. We're going to paper one wall in the spare bedroom, set up Julia's big girl bed in there, and move the rest of her toys and furniture in there. We're planning to put her to bed in her new room tomorrow night. It's time she moved out of the nursery."

"That sounds good." She arched a brow at Susan. "Any plans for the nursery?"

Aaron joined them and put his arm around his wife's shoulders. He and Susan looked at each other and smiled.

"There's nothing to report—yet—but we're ready for number two."

Maggie clasped her hands together. "I was hoping you'd say that."

"Back to your original question," Susan continued. "We

think we'll finish the room today. If we do, we'll sleep in and go for a hike tomorrow. Maybe hit brunch at Pete's."

"We might take in a matinee movie," Aaron said. "If you don't mind keeping Julia that long."

John was hopping back and forth over the threshold with Julia, oblivious to everyone else.

"That'll be fine. Take all the time you need. Have you ever wallpapered before?"

Susan and Aaron shook their heads.

"We've watched videos about how to do it," Aaron said. "How hard can it be?"

Maggie opened her mouth to reply. Depending on the pattern on the paper, it could be harder than it looked. She thought better of it and remained silent.

"I showed you what we picked, didn't I?" Susan reached into her bag and removed her phone. She scrolled until she found the photo she was looking for. "Here—this is what we chose."

Maggie tapped at the screen and expanded the photo. "Green leaves with flowers in all the primary and secondary colors. A wise choice. It's cute without being babyish. You can use any of the flower colors as accents."

"That's the plan. I hope she'll be happy with this for years."

"The only thing I have on my calendar is to take food to Frank and Loretta and the kids," Maggie continued. "Tomorrow is my turn."

"What're you taking?"

"Chicken in sauce casserole, rice, and cherry Waldorf

jello salad," Maggie said. "Nothing spicy for the nursing mom. And a big batch of chocolate chip cookies."

"I love that meal," Susan said.

"Why don't you plan to come to dinner tomorrow night? I'll make a double batch of everything. You can leave Julia with us until you come for dinner."

Susan glanced at Aaron, who nodded. "That's really nice of you, Mom. We'd love to do that."

"I should be home from dropping off food by 4:45, at the latest." Maggie sighed wistfully. "I can't wait to see those babies."

"They're so sweet. I see a lot of Frank in both of them," Susan said.

"How's it going over there?"

"So far, so good. As you know, I've been driving the kids to school every morning. They tell me that the babies are getting up every two and a half to three hours to eat, but they must go right back to sleep because their crying hasn't woken any of the kids."

"Whoa," Maggie said. "That's brutal. And she's nursing exclusively?"

"Yep. No formula. Frank's been home all week to change diapers and help get them back to sleep. And dinner's been provided every night. All of that's helped."

"I take my hat off to them," Maggie said. "I remember how difficult it was when your brother's twins were newborns. Frank and Loretta will need a nanny and house cleaners."

"I'm sure they will," Susan said. She looked toward the

front door. John was on his hands and knees, acting out the animal when Julia made the sound associated with it. "I'd say goodbye, but I don't think she'll care if we leave or not."

"Actually, could you come inside for a minute? I have something to show you and ask you."

"Go ahead," Aaron said. "We've got plenty of time."

Susan climbed the stone steps to the arched door.

John stood, brushing the dust from his knees and looking sheepish. "Let's go inside and find Roman and Eve," he said to Julia. "They're in the garden." He extended his hand to Aaron, and they shook. "Could you use a cup of coffee?"

"Always," Aaron said.

"Let's grab one on the way to the garden. We can sit on the patio and watch this one," he pointed to Julia, "chase Roman and Eve."

"I wonder who will wear out first," Aaron said.

"My money's on Julia to outlast both of them." They headed toward the kitchen.

"What've you got to show me?" Susan asked her mother.

"Do you remember that vintage Dior coat that David and Sean found at Westbury Animal Hospital?" Maggie led them to the stairway.

"The red one that had been in John's lost and found for decades? With a diamond Van Cleef & Arpels brooch pinned to the lapel, no less."

"That's the one. Gordon Mortimer forwarded me the advertisement for the auction where the brooch will be sold next month. It reminded me of the coat, so I dug it out of the back of my closet." They climbed to the second floor.

"I put it on this morning, and I don't really like it."

"Doesn't it fit? You could have it altered."

"It's not that. I don't know. There's something about it that just isn't me. I wondered if you'd like to have it?"

"I remember it being beautifully made. It's dressy, too."

"You could wear it to the office," Maggie said. "You still wear business attire when you go to your law office, don't you?"

They entered Maggie and John's bedroom. The designer coat was spread out across the foot of the bed.

Maggie reached for it and held it out for Susan to try on.

Susan slipped her arms through the sleeves and buttoned the oversize buttons. She turned to the full-length mirror on the wall. "The color is gorgeous, but it doesn't fit." She lifted both arms. "The armholes are far too tight. I feel like I can't move."

Maggie ran her hands across the fabric between her daughter's shoulder blades. "You're too tall," she said. "I'm not sure if it could be altered to fit you."

Susan turned from side to side, admiring the coat in the mirror.

"We could take it to Archer's. Anita could do it if anyone could."

"Someone who loves vintage clothing would adore this coat. It's gorgeous. It needs to be worn." She dropped her arms to her sides and swung to face her mother.

"Amy!" both women cried in unison.

"Why didn't I think of her before?" Maggie put her hand

to the side of her head. "She loves vintage pieces and this shade of red is her color."

"And she's a good six inches shorter than me. I'll bet it'll fit her perfectly." Susan unbuttoned the coat. "I'm sure she'll go nuts over this!"

Maggie took the coat from Susan and hung it safely in the closet. "That's a load off my mind. I'll mail it to her next week," she said. "Now—let's get you and that husband of yours on your way. I hope I'm wrong, but I think you may have a big project ahead of you."

MAGGIE SLID onto the sofa next to John. Roman was curled into a ball at his feet and Eve was snoozing in her basket by the hearth. A baseball game was playing on the television, but John wasn't paying attention.

She touched his arm lightly and his eyes flew open. "What... oh... I guess I dozed off. Is Julia asleep?"

"Finally," Maggie said, bringing her hand up to cover a yawn.

"I got her all riled up, didn't I?"

"Chasing her from one end of the second floor to the other at bedtime isn't a wise idea," Maggie said.

"Sorry. She wanted to."

"You can say no to her, you know." Maggie arched a brow at him.

"I... well... next time," John said sheepishly. "What would

you like to do now? Is there something you'd like to watch?" He picked up the remote to change the channel.

"Honestly? I'm bushed—and I know you are too. Let's call it a night. Julia still gets up at the crack of dawn, so we can't sleep in."

"Sounds good to me. I'm so used to being at the hospital for surgery at six that I can never sleep in, anyway. If she wakes early, I'll get up with her. You can stay in bed." He stood and pulled Maggie to her feet.

Roman stretched.

Maggie patted her leg to signal to Eve that it was time to go out.

The two humans and their four-legged companions ambled to the kitchen and out the door to the back garden. Roman and Eve raced ahead to their favorite spots on the lawn.

"Will you share the surgical duties with the new veterinarian you've hired?"

"That's my long-term plan. I'll observe Dr. Parker with our patients—both human and animal—before I turn anything over."

"She comes highly recommended, doesn't she? Top of her veterinary school class, if I remember."

"That's right. She starts in a month. I hope I'll feel comfortable enough with her by the end of the summer to cut back my hours."

Maggie slipped her arm into his. "I intend to hold you to that, my love. You work far too hard."

"If that isn't the pot calling the kettle black." He whistled for the dogs and they came at a trot.

"Duly noted," Maggie replied. "Let's take these guys upstairs and hit the hay. We can debate which one of us is the harder worker tomorrow."

CHAPTER 9

Maggie tracked down John and Julia at the stone wall at the bottom of the garden. "What're you up to?"

"We're examining this wall for any cracks that developed over the winter. My favorite gal loves to sit here with her morning coffee until the first frost."

Julia ran from one end of the wall to the other, Roman and Eve at her heels.

John stood and planted a kiss on the top of Maggie's head. "If it needs any repairs, I'll get to it."

She turned to look at the rear façade of Rosemont, perched at the top of the sloping lawn. "Maintaining this old beauty is a lot of work. All of that falls on you, and I want you to know how much I appreciate everything you do."

"No big deal," John said, flushing with pleasure at her

remark. "You've got your purse on your shoulder. Are you going somewhere?"

"I'm taking dinner to Frank's family. I'm running ten minutes behind schedule. Susan and Aaron are coming for an early dinner at a quarter to five. I won't be home by then."

"We'll keep an eye out for them," John said. "Julia and I can go out front. She loves to play on the steps."

Maggie knelt and intercepted her granddaughter as she ran toward them. "Would you like to draw on the driveway out front? We've got great big sidewalk chalk for you to use. You can make a picture for your mommy and daddy."

Julia nodded.

Maggie took her hand, and they walked up the hill.

"Where's this chalk?" John asked as they stepped onto the patio.

"On the counter in the laundry room," Maggie said. "That should keep our girl busy for quite a while." She bent to Julia. "You be a good girl for grandpa. I'll be back soon, and your parents will be here shortly."

Julia placed her hand into John's, and they headed for the chalk.

Maggie went to the garage and was soon on her way to Frank and Loretta's. The heady aroma of warm chocolate chip cookies mingled with the smell of the chicken casserole. Her mouth watered. This would be a good meal.

She pulled into the driveway at four thirteen and hurried to the door.

Marissa opened it before she could ring the bell. "Hi," she said softly. "Mom and the babies are asleep."

"We wouldn't want to wake them," Maggie whispered, stuffing down her disappointment that she wouldn't see Bonnie or Branson. She took a deep breath. The babies weren't going anywhere and she'd signed up to bring dinner the following Sunday. She'd meet them then.

"Do you need help with anything?" Marissa asked.

Maggie handed her the glass bowl that contained the jello salad. "Can you put this in the fridge and come out to my car? The two of us can bring in the rest."

Marissa did as Maggie requested and joined her at the car.

Maggie handed her a large ceramic bowl containing cooked jasmine rice. "It's warm. Are you okay with it?"

"I've got it."

Maggie put on oven mitts and grabbed the hot baking dish containing the chicken chunks nestled in a cream sauce. She balanced the plate of cookies on top of the baking dish and kicked the car door shut with her foot.

"That smells wonderful," Marissa said. "It's so nice of everyone to make us food."

"Have you enjoyed it?"

"Everything's been great. We have enough leftovers for lunch the next day, too."

She led them into the kitchen. "We'll be back to fast food or DoorDash when the meals run out."

Maggie turned on the wall oven to two hundred degrees and slipped the chicken in to stay warm. "How's everything going?"

"The babies need to be fed every three hours—around the

clock. All Mom does is nurse them and try to sleep for a few hours until they need to eat again. Frank burps them and changes diapers, and then he tries to sleep. It's all we do around here. I change diapers once in a while, but I spend most of my time taking care of Nicole."

"I'm sure it's overwhelming right now. Things will get better. It won't be this all-consuming forever." Maggie took off her oven mitts and patted Marissa's elbow. "It sounds like you've been a tremendous help. I know your mom and Frank appreciate that. What about Sean? Does he help?"

"He's at the shelter every chance he gets. I think he's afraid to touch Bonnie and Branson. I've told him he can't hurt them, but he still won't. He's spending most of his free time with David and Dodger—and he's having a ball."

Maggie leaned against the counter. "Have you spent time with your friends?"

Marissa shook her head. "I see them at school and we eat lunch together, but that's it. I dropped out of my jazz dance troupe because I don't want to be away from home two nights a week."

"Do your mom or Frank know you did that?"

Marissa shrugged. "I didn't tell them. I don't want them to feel bad. And I want to help with my sister and brother. They're so sweet. I love them."

"Of course you do, but you need to continue with your own interests. And see your friends."

"It'll be fine," Marissa said.

Maggie looked at the clock on the oven. "I'd better go. Susan and Aaron are coming for dinner." She noticed stacks of clean bowls and casserole dishes on the far end of the kitchen island. "What are those?"

"They're the clean dishes we need to return to people who've brought us meals. Frank is going to drop them off—when he can."

"I'm happy to do that for you. Can you tell me who they belong to?"

"I've written a thank you note to each person," Marissa said. "The notes are nestled inside the top dish in each stack."

"That's very efficient of you," Maggie said. "I'll be glad to get them out of your hair. Help me carry them to my car and I'll be on my way."

Maggie and Marissa stowed all the clean dishes in Maggie's back seat.

"Thanks again, Ms. Martin," Marissa said.

Maggie faced the girl. "You're extremely responsible and very helpful. Those are wonderful things and you should be very proud. But remember, you're still a kid. You need your friends—and your dance troupe. Your parents won't want you to sacrifice these things. Talk to them. They'll understand."

Marissa pursed her lips. "You think so?"

"I do."

Marissa nodded as Maggie got into her car.

"Things will get better. They really will," Maggie said before pulling out of the driveway and heading home.

CHAPTER 10

"Gordon." Maggie answered her phone as she got out of her car and headed for her office after lunch.

"Good afternoon, madam." Gordon Mortimer kept his formal style of speech, despite the friendship he and Maggie had formed during their prior business dealings. "I hope this is a good time."

"It's perfect. I have thirty minutes before my next meeting. To what do I owe this pleasure?"

"I wanted to make sure you saw the advertisement for the auction in London next month."

"I did. The write-up and photo of the brooch are excellent. I wish we could be present." Her heels tapped against the stone steps leading to the entrance of the ornate red brick administration building of Highpointe College, where her office as president was located.

"I'll be in London on another matter and will attend on your behalf. It's the most beautiful piece being offered, in my opinion. I'm very hopeful it'll bring a handsome price."

"John and I are, too. With all the proceeds going to establish a service dog training school in Westbury, we need every dollar we can get."

"I'm gratified to hear you still intend to donate the proceeds. As I said before, I'm going to waive my commission."

"That's very kind of you, Gordon. I remember you have a favorite cousin who uses a seeing eye dog. He'll be very pleased to know you're supporting our venture."

"That's the other reason I'm calling. I'm visiting my cousin at the end of the month—right before I leave for London. He lives about two hours from Westbury. I was wondering if I could drop by to collect that Thomas Cole painting from your attic. It needs professional cleaning—and possibly restoration—before we send it to auction."

"That would be wonderful," Maggie said. "Can you spend a day or two with us to check out the remaining furniture in the attic? Remember—you promised you'd stay with us at Rosemont when you came back."

"I'd hate to inconvenience—"

"Nonsense," Maggie interrupted him. "John and I have been looking forward to having you. Spend as much time here as you need. You've been in a tearing hurry on all of your other visits. We'd like you to slow down and relax."

Gordon hesitated before he continued. "If you really don't mind?"

"Not at all."

"Then I'd like to spend three days with you. That should give me time to assess the antique furniture. And to take another look at the rare stamp we found taped to the bottom of the desk on my last visit."

"I'd forgotten about that. I put it in our safe as soon as you left—as you told me to. It's been there ever since."

"Good. That's the best place for it. Leave it there until I arrive."

Maggie raced to her desk, nodding to Josh Newlon, her administrative assistant, as she passed. "Let me write down when you'll be here." She crossed to her desk and grabbed a pen from the lap drawer. She opened her calendar. "Okay... shoot."

Gordon gave her the dates of his visit.

"Great," Maggie said. "I don't have conflicts on any of those dates." She sank into her desk chair and leaned back. "Are you by any chance interested in rare books?" she asked, tapping her pen against her calendar.

"My interest is personal, rather than professional. I have a modest collection of my own. The rare book world is complex and full of dealers and academicians with extensive expertise. If you have rare books you want to have assessed, I can put you in touch with someone with the requisite experience. It wouldn't be me."

"I don't believe I have any rare books at Rosemont. Not anymore. Hector Martin collected them, but he donated all his books to the Highpointe College Library before he died."

"Hector was the one who acquired all that silver we

auctioned off—including the Martin-Guillaume Biennais tea set. What a masterpiece. Hector had quite an eye."

"He certainly did—and I'm the benefactor of most of it. His rare book collection led us to the former rare-book librarian from Cambridge University. It's a very long story, but he lives in Westbury now. I think the two of you would enjoy meeting. Would it be all right if I hosted a small dinner party for you while you're here?"

"Madam… that would be most kind."

"I'll include the rare-book librarian from Highpointe, too. Perhaps you'd like to tour our collection while you're here?"

"Absolutely!"

Maggie smiled to herself. The only other time she'd heard happy excitement in Gordon's voice was when he'd discovered the Martin-Guillaume Biennais tea set in her attic.

"Terrific. This time, when you come to Rosemont, you'll have some fun. And I remember your allergy to cats, so I'll board Blossom, Bubbles, and Buttercup."

"I hate to put you to that trouble."

"It'll be fine. Since John owns Westbury Animal Hospital, it'll be easy to house them there for a few days."

"Thank you, madam, for all of your kindness."

"Don't mention it." She glanced at the dates written on her calendar. "See you in three weeks, Gordon. I can't wait."

Maggie smiled as she ended the call. As soon as she was done with her next meeting, she'd contact Highpointe's rare-book librarian and Cambridge's former rare-book librarian. She was sure Sunday Sloan and Robert Harris would jump at the chance to discuss their favorite topic with Gordon over dinner at Rosemont.

CHAPTER 11

"*A*re you sure you'll be all right by yourself?" Frank shifted his weight from foot to foot as he stood in the doorway to their bedroom.

Loretta stuffed her feet into her slippers and joined him.

"We've gotta go. I can't be late to first period," Marissa called from the end of the hallway.

"I'll be fine. Ingrid will be here any minute now," Loretta said.

"But you said last night you wanted to shower and dress before she got here."

"Branson took too long to nurse. It's fine. I'll shower later."

"Frank!" Marissa called again.

"I can come back, if you'd like."

"Not on your life. Get the kids to school and go to work.

I'm sure that with both of us out last week, Haynes Enterprises could use your attention."

Frank brushed her cheek with a kiss. "Call me if you need anything."

"Don't worry. I'm fine here. I can carry on as I've been doing for the past week. Nursing babies, burping babies, changing babies, and getting them back to sleep."

Frank tucked a strand of hair behind her ear, then turned and strode down the hall to the garage.

Loretta retrieved her full cup of cold coffee from the nightstand and padded to the kitchen. She dumped the contents down the sink and fixed herself a hot cup.

For the first time in a week, the house was completely quiet.

She brought the steaming liquid to her lips and blew across the top. The pungent aroma filled her nose, and she inhaled slowly. When it was cool enough to drink, she took a sip. The warmth traveling down her throat was comforting.

Loretta moved to the living room window and stood in a pool of sunshine, savoring the simple pleasure of drinking a cup of coffee uninterrupted. She'd just drained her cup when she saw the sturdy woman of middle years approaching from the other side of the street.

Ingrid looked to be ten years older than Loretta. She'd worked as a pediatric ICU nurse until the physical and emotional demands of the job had become too much for her. She had four adult children of her own, a wealth of experience with babies, and expertise as a lactation consultant. Her hourly rate was double that of the other nanny candidates they'd interviewed, but Ingrid was their top choice. Frank had insisted they could afford her.

Loretta set her empty cup on the nearest table and went to the door. She opened it as Ingrid was pulling out her phone to text Loretta. Ingrid had suggested this procedure so that she wouldn't wake sleeping babies by knocking or ringing the doorbell.

"Good morning," Loretta said. "I'm glad to see you."

"Sorry I'm late," Ingrid said. "I take the bus, and it ran behind schedule."

"Not a problem. I don't have anywhere to go."

"Your husband has gone back to work?"

"He has. This morning."

"How are you?" Ingrid set her purse on the entry table and took her lunch sack to the kitchen.

Loretta followed her. "I'm doing okay—I think."

Ingrid looked at her with kind eyes. "I'd like to hear about last week."

Loretta filled her in on the details.

"Sounds like you're handling Bonnie and Branson extremely well. I'm glad they were so big at birth and you didn't have to come home without them. That's a nightmare for parents."

Loretta nodded.

"You've told me about the babies. What about you?"

"I'm exhausted, of course. That's to be expected. And I need a shower." She ran her hand down her rumpled bathrobe. "I'd planned to be dressed before you got here, but getting my other three off to school and feeding the twins—well..." She smiled ruefully.

"You've already done a lot before I arrived. I thought we could work on a schedule together this morning. I'd suggest you take an hour to yourself as soon as I'm here. You can shower, read, journal—whatever would make you feel grounded to start your day."

Loretta put a hand on her chest. "That sounds wonderful."

"How are your other kids reacting? Sometimes it's hard to see so much of their mother's attention devoted to the newborn—in your case, newborns."

"Sean is spending most of his time with friends, and Marissa—she's the oldest—has been very good about taking care of Nicole."

"And your husband? How's he coping?"

"He stayed home all last week and was a champ with the babies. He burped them after they nursed and changed almost every diaper." She sighed. "He went back to work today, and I feel sorry for him. He hasn't had any more sleep than I've had. I don't know how he's going to concentrate on his job."

"You'd be surprised how relaxing it can be for people to return to work after they've had a baby. Whether it's a mother or a father, returning to work can be a welcome distraction from the never-ending demands of a new baby."

"I hadn't thought of it like that. Bonnie and Branson command all my attention."

"As they should—at least for now."

Ingrid pointed to the baby monitor that stood on the kitchen counter. "They're fast asleep."

Loretta nodded. "But not for long." She checked the clock on the wall oven. "They'll probably be up in thirty minutes."

"Why don't you go take your shower?"

"What if they wake early? Should I wait until after the next feeding?"

Ingrid smiled and put her hand on Loretta's back. "I'm sure I can handle them for a few minutes if you're in the shower. If we're going to get them on a schedule, we should start now."

Loretta released a slow breath. Ingrid was exactly the person they needed in their lives. She walked purposefully toward her bedroom.

"And don't rush," Ingrid called after her. "Taking care of yourself is good for your whole family."

CHAPTER 12

Frank Haynes sprinted up the steps to Haynes Enterprises. The lights were on in the small reception area outside his office, and Mary—the efficient administrative assistant they'd hired to assist Loretta—was tapping away at her keyboard.

"Morning, Frank," she said as she jumped out of her chair and rushed to him. She brought her arms up to hug him but thought better of it. "Congratulations!"

"Thank you, Mary." Frank halted on his way to his office and forced himself to be sociable. He'd never been very good at it and had promised Loretta he'd be friendly to Mary. Loretta liked the young single mother and wanted her to remain at Haynes Enterprises. Even when Loretta returned to work, she only planned to keep part-time hours. Mary was a quick study, and both Frank and Loretta knew Mary would become a valuable member of their team.

"How are the babies?"

"They're…" Frank searched for words. "Remarkable." He whipped out his phone and opened his photos. He turned the screen to Mary and pride washed over him like a palpable force.

"Oh… They're adorable!" She smiled at Frank.

He turned and stood next to her as he scrolled to the next picture.

"So big!" Mary said.

He summoned the next picture, and the next.

"Look at all that hair."

Frank kept scrolling.

"You've certainly been busy with your camera, haven't you?" Mary asked the rhetorical question.

"They're really something, aren't they?"

"How is it having twins?"

"Loretta feeds them both at the same time. They eat and go right back to sleep. They're so good."

"How often?"

"Every three hours."

Mary took a step back. "OMG. How is Loretta doing?"

"She's hanging in there."

"I can't imagine."

"We hired a nanny to help during the day while I'm at work."

"I'm glad to hear it. Please tell Loretta I'm thinking of her. And that she trained me very well and I'm keeping things caught up here at work."

"She'll be relieved to hear it. Speaking of work—I'd better

get to my desk. Did anything urgent come in last week that I need to attend to first thing?"

"Tim Knudsen dropped off a contract on Friday for you to review. It's for the sale of the final condos in Florida."

"The ones that the town workers' pension fund had listed for sale?"

"Yes. That's what Tim said. He's hoping you can look at the contract before tomorrow evening's town council meeting. Consideration of the contract is on the agenda."

Frank nodded.

"There's a stack of phone messages for you to return, and I've sorted the mail into three folders. One is invoices, one is business correspondence, and one is junk mail."

"Thank you, Mary. That sounds very efficient. Please call Tim to tell him I'll look at the contract as soon as I can—definitely before the council meeting." Frank opened the door to the office where, until he'd married Loretta, he'd spent eighteen hours a day working to build his fast-food franchise business into a multi-million dollar enterprise.

He flipped on the overhead lights, opened the blinds, and slipped into his seat with choreographed precision. Frank logged into his computer and was about to check the bank account balances when he stopped short. The manufacturer's desktop image of a mountain rising from the ocean would no longer greet him every time he sat down to work. He knew dozens of people who used photos of their kids as their desktop images. Frank was going to become one of those people.

He googled "how to upload photo as desktop image" and

read the instructions. It didn't sound hard. He opened the photos on his phone and scrolled back and forth until he selected one he'd taken the prior afternoon of Loretta in the rocking chair holding the babies, with Marissa, Sean, and Nicole hovering over them from behind.

It was a lovely photo of his beautiful family. Warmth surged from his fingertips to his toes. Frank transferred the photo to his computer and followed the instructions. His oversize monitor was soon filled with the image.

He leaned back in his chair and stared at the smiling faces in front of him. Frank bit his lip. Thoughts of his felony convictions—always in the front of his mind—swirled in his brain. Would his children one day hate him for the mistakes he'd made? They deserved better than him, that much he knew.

Frank blinked rapidly. He couldn't change the past. All he could do was be the best man he could be now. His strong suit was running a successful business. He knew how to negotiate a deal and make money.

He'd served the community service portion of his sentence as an advisor to the town workers' pension fund. He'd been instrumental in helping sell assets that restored the fund's solvency. That's why Tim and the council wanted his opinion of this contract that would benefit the fund.

Frank tore his eyes from the people who meant everything to him and picked up the stack of phone messages. He'd work his way through them, then turn his attention to the bulging folder labeled "Invoices." Haynes Enterprises was never late on its payments to vendors and it wouldn't start now.

When he finished those, he'd sort through the correspondence and then turn his attention to the contract Tim had dropped off. With any luck, he'd be done by mid-afternoon and surprise Loretta by getting home early.

Frank bent his head to his task and was finishing the invoices when Mary knocked lightly on the door frame to his office.

"I'll be leaving now, Frank. I wanted to say goodnight."

Frank's head shot up. "You're leaving?"

"It's after 5:30," Mary said.

Frank's head snapped to his watch. "I had no idea. I've lost all track of time."

"You've been working like mad all day," Mary agreed.

"Have a good evening," he said. "Please lock the door on your way out."

"Are you going to be here for a while?"

Frank's shoulders drooped. "I'm afraid I'll have to be. I haven't even looked at the correspondence yet, let alone the contract for the council."

Mary opened her mouth to speak, then closed it again. If Frank wanted to stay late on his first day back, it was none of her business.

Frank picked up the file marked "Correspondence" and set it in the center of his desk. He reached for his phone to call Loretta and thought better of it. He didn't want to interrupt her or wake the babies. Frank tapped out a brief text message, telling her he was still trying to catch up and that he'd be home by seven. Eight at the latest. They shouldn't wait for him for dinner.

Frank pressed send and immersed himself in his work.

CHAPTER 13

Maggie got out of her car in the parking lot behind the Highpointe College Library as two familiar figures came out of the employee entrance. She waved her hand over her head to gain their attention.

"President Martin," Sunday called in response.

"Maggie, please," Maggie said as she walked up to Sunday Sloan, the rare-book librarian at Highpointe and Lyla Kershaw, the library's general administrator.

"Maggie, then," Sunday said. "It feels odd to be calling the president of the college by her first name."

"I prefer it," Maggie said. "Formal titles have a time and place, but this isn't one of them."

"Is there something we can help you with—in the library?" Lyla asked.

"I'm here to see both of you," Maggie said. "I'd like you—

and Josh and Robert, if they're available—to come to Rose-mont for dinner a week from Wednesday."

Lyla and Sunday looked at each other, then turned back to Maggie. "Robert and I would love to," Lyla said.

"Same for me and Josh."

"Don't you need to ask them first?"

"We never have plans on a weeknight," Lyla said.

"We don't either," Sunday chimed in.

"Excellent. I know we'll all be coming from work. Shall we gather at 6:00 and plan to sit down to dinner at 6:30?"

"That'll be perfect," Sunday said. "Can I bring anything? Is this some sort of working dinner for the library?"

"No. This is a purely social occasion. Our auctioneer friend will be in town and he's staying with us. Gordon has a personal interest in rare books. I thought he'd enjoy meeting Robert and Sunday."

Sunday clasped her hands together. "That'll be so much fun. I'd love to give him a tour of the Highpointe collection, too."

"I told him as much and he's very excited about it."

"Are you sure you want to subject everyone to an evening with three rare-book enthusiasts? Once we get going, you won't be able to shut us up. It could make for deadly dull dinner conversation." Sunday wrung her hands.

Maggie chuckled. "I'm prepared to take that risk." She looked at Lyla. "I'm sure Lyla and Josh can entertain John and me by telling us about their latest paintings."

Lyla cocked her head to one side. "You know that he and I both paint?"

"I do. And that you and Josh became friends during a painting class long before you ever learned that you're his birth mother. The story of your reunion is one of the most joyful things I've ever heard."

Lyla blushed.

"Gordon is an expert in American painters," Maggie said. "He's coming to collect what we believe is an original Thomas Cole from our attic."

Lyla gasped. "*The* Thomas Cole?"

Maggie nodded. "It used to be over the mantel in the living room. It needs to be cleaned and authenticated."

"Will you hang it again when that's done?"

"No. John and I are raising money to fund a service dog training school in Westbury. If the Cole is worth what Gordon thinks it is, selling it will move us a long way toward that goal. Gordon will place it in an auction for us."

"That's kind of you and John," Lyla said.

"Gordon is donating his commission to the school on any of the items we sell to raise money," Maggie said.

"That's very generous of him," Sunday said.

"Anyway—he'll be staying at Rosemont for a few days while he combs through the attic. He's been up there briefly a few times before and noticed several pieces of furniture he thinks may be valuable. We may have more things we can sell to raise money."

"How intriguing. I must say, your attic sounds fascinating," Sunday said.

"Believe me, it is," Maggie said. "It's settled. See you next week. It looks like you were on your way out. I'm sorry to hold you up."

"We've got plenty of time to run our errand," Lyla said. "We're headed to Celebrations to pick up a baby gift—or, rather, baby gifts. I'm taking dinner tonight to Loretta and Frank. I wanted to bring a small present."

"I invited myself to go along," Sunday said. "I love going to that store."

"Judy certainly knows how to merchandise," Maggie said. "It's my favorite shop in town. They have a terrific selection of children's books. My husband is in there every week, buying a new one for our granddaughter."

"As a librarian, I love the sound of that!" Sunday chuckled.

"Books," Lyla said. "That's a great idea. We'll pick out books for the babies."

Lyla and Sunday nodded in agreement.

"It's very nice of you to do this for them. I didn't know you were friends," Maggie said.

"We're not, really. More like friends of friends. Everyone was so kind to us when Josh got out of the hospital and recuperated at my house—I want to pay it forward. Besides, my husband does all the cooking and he's very excited to be making a big family meal."

"Robert's wonderful in the kitchen. He always sends food to Josh," Sunday said.

"He's really excited about the meal he's making for Frank and Loretta. Robert spent the weekend combing through recipes on the New York Times website. He's changed his mind at least a dozen times. I'm not sure what he finally decided on."

"I'm sure it'll be delicious," Sunday said.

"My mouth is watering, just hearing about all the effort he's putting into this," Maggie said.

"If there's one thing I've learned about Westbury," Sunday said, "it's that people go all out for each other."

The three women smiled at each other in agreement.

MAGGIE DROVE BACK to the imposing Administration Building and parked in front of the bronze placard emblazoned with the word "President." She checked her watch. With a full thirty minutes before her next conference call, she could take a break.

She ambled along the sidewalks crisscrossing the quadrangle that stretched in front of the building. Students—arms laden with laptops and books—hurried past her, their heads down and thoughts undoubtedly on upcoming exams. A gentle breeze chased high clouds in a brilliant blue sky. Birds tittered in the trees that dotted the paths.

Maggie inhaled deeply the sweet aroma of spring. She stepped off the sidewalk to claim a seat on a vacant bench shaded by a canopy of fresh green leaves. The aura of hope and expectancy that pervaded a college campus at this time of year quickened her pulse. She surveyed the scene around her and knew there was nowhere she'd rather be.

When she'd been married to her late husband, the former

president of Windsor College, she'd felt the same sort of joyful anticipation whenever she set foot on campus. Maggie had never dreamed she'd fill the role of college president, but now that she had, she knew she was where she belonged.

Her cell phone rang in her purse. She churned through the contents and grabbed it. The caller ID told her Judy Young was calling. She swiped to answer the call just before it went to voicemail.

"Judy," Maggie said. "Hi."

"I was just getting ready to leave you a message," Judy said. "Do you have a minute?"

Maggie took another look at her watch. "I have ten minutes, actually."

"Good. I won't take that much of your time. I was calling to ask if Jeff and I could stop by Rosemont to meet Gordon Mortimer while he's staying with you."

"How do you know about Gordon?"

"Sunday and Lyla were just in Celebrations. They told me."

Maggie brushed her hair off of her shoulders. "That's right. They were headed your way."

"If it's not convenient, I completely understand," Judy rushed to add.

"It's fine. Of course you can stop by. You were so helpful with the silver we found in the attic. You told me it was valuable. Gordon knows all about you. He'll be thrilled to meet you."

"That's so nice to hear. I had no idea you'd mentioned me to him."

"I most certainly did."

"I'd like to see if he'd look at some things we've found in the attic of the Olsson house. Jeff suspects some of it might be valuable. We don't think we'll have anything nearly as nice as you've found in the Rosemont attic," she hastened to add.

"I hope you've got even more valuable stuff up there," Maggie said. "Gordon is the perfect person to help you figure all that out. I'm sure he'll be eager to look."

Judy sighed heavily. "That's a relief. I know we can trust him."

"He may not be able to go through your attic while he's in town next week," Maggie said.

"That's fine. We're not ready for him to get into the attic now, anyway. Jeff is restoring the place, top to bottom. The interior is down to the studs while the plumbing and electrical are being replaced. The stairway to the attic needs to be rebuilt. Jeff doesn't want anyone using those steps until that's done. We'd like to introduce ourselves and schedule him to come to the Olsson house another time."

Maggie chuckled.

"What's so funny?"

"I was just picturing Gordon's face when he learns Westbury has another historic home with an attic that's potentially full of treasures." She took a breath and composed herself. "I wouldn't be surprised if he asked Tim Knudsen to find him an old home to buy. I'm sure Gordon would love to own an attic full of abandoned treasures."

"It's always been a fantasy of mine," Judy admitted.

"Mine, too," Maggie said.

"And now—we've both done it. Imagine that!"

"Life is interesting, that's for sure. I never imagined that my late husband hid his ownership of a historic mansion in a far-away town—and that I would inherit it when he died suddenly. Life's full of unexpected twists and turns."

"You can say that again. Who would have thought I would buy the Olsson house at a tax sale? Or that a box of hand-carved ornaments I found in the attic would lead me to the love of my life."

"Jeff is your destiny, just as Rosemont was mine. Without Rosemont, I wouldn't have adopted Eve on my first night in the house and I'd never have met John when I took her to the vet."

"These houses, Maggie—they bestow special benedictions and graces on us. Jeff thinks I'm kooky in the way I feel about the Olsson house, but I know you understand."

"I absolutely do. I couldn't agree with you more." Maggie told Judy the dates of Gordon's visit. "In fact," Maggie said, "why don't you and Jeff come to dinner at Rosemont next Wednesday night? I'm throwing a small dinner party for Gordon."

"That's so nice—we'd be delighted."

"Perfect. It'll be the ideal time to meet him."

"How small is this 'small' party?" Judy asked.

Maggie tallied the count in her head. "With you and Jeff, we'll be nine."

Judy whistled softly. "I guess nine people for dinner is small for Rosemont."

"It'll be fun. We're looking forward to it."

CHAPTER 14

*F*rank stepped out of his office, clutching a neat stack of invoices. He walked to Mary's desk, where she was pulling her purse out of her bottom desk drawer.

"You're leaving?" he asked.

"It's after five," she replied, pointing over her shoulder to the clock on the wall. She held out her hand to take the invoices from him.

Frank released them before she had a good grasp on them, and they tumbled to the floor. He drew in a sharp breath.

"Oh, sorry," Mary said. "That was clumsy of me." She dropped to one knee and scooped the papers together, depositing them on her desk in an unruly pile. "I'll file these first thing in the morning." She gave him a bright smile.

Frank scowled in return.

Mary didn't notice. "Are you coming too? I'll bet you're eager to get home to those babies."

"I'm nowhere near caught up yet," he snapped. "I'll be here for hours."

"Oh… I'm sorry." She set her purse on her desk. "Do you need me to stay? I'll call my mom to see if she can pick up my kids from their after-school program." Her eagerness to please was written across her face.

Frank swallowed hard. "No. Of course not. Have a good night."

"If you're sure?" Mary put her purse on her shoulder.

"I'll see you tomorrow." Frank walked her to the door and locked it behind her. He didn't know why he was so irritable lately. Mary was a hard worker and a fast learner. Loretta had loved working with her before the babies had been born, and Frank could see why.

Frank yawned and stretched his arms over his head. He was exhausted. Getting up in the middle of the night every night to help with the babies must be getting to him. That's why he was so cranky.

He passed Mary's desk as he returned to his office. He reached his door, then swung around and went back to her desk.

Frank picked up the loose pile of invoices and tidied them into a neat stack. He set them down, and the corner of one piece of paper in the middle of the stack stuck out a quarter inch. Frank picked up the pile and fussed with the papers until every edge was perfectly aligned. He carefully replaced the stack on the desk, squaring the corners, before placing a stapler on top to secure it.

He leaned back and studied her desk. The phone cord was tangled in a loopy mess and an uncapped pen lay in the middle of the desk. A shiver ran down his spine.

There was nothing wrong with the way Mary kept her desk. No one would find it offensive, he told himself. He capped the pen and placed it in a cylindrical container on the corner of her desk before spending a minute or two restoring order to her phone cord.

Frank inhaled deeply as he regarded the results of his efforts. Pens and pencils were intermingled in the container. He was segregating them when his cell phone began to ring in his office. The ringtone told him it was Loretta. He abandoned his task and hurried down the hall to answer.

"Yeah," he said as he brought the phone to his ear.

"Well… Hello to you, too," Loretta said.

"Sorry… I'm sorry. I was tidying Mary's desk and had to run to get the phone."

"Tidying her desk? Why? She was always neat as a pin."

Frank's eyebrow twitched. "You're not calling to check on Mary's desk," he said. "What do you want?"

"Okay, Mr. Grumpy Pants. I'm calling to see when you'll be home. We just finished dinner—Joan brought us the best chicken thighs I've ever eaten—and I want to know whether to put a plate for you in the oven to stay warm."

Frank rubbed his temple with his left hand. Why was he being so snippy with everyone? Especially Loretta? "I'll be here for at least another couple of hours."

"I'll put the leftovers in the fridge," Loretta said. "Did you have lunch?"

Frank was silent.

"I didn't think so. You've got to be starving, sweetheart. At least run across the street to get yourself a burger. You know the owner of the restaurant," she teased. "Seriously, working all the time, skipping meals, and not getting an uninterrupted night's sleep will take a toll on you. I understand you need to get caught up at work and we can't change when the babies wake up, but what you eat is under your control."

Frank knew she was right. "Don't nag me, Loretta," he heard himself retort.

"I'm tired, too, Frank. I don't need you biting my head off. Go do what you've got to do. Just know this: tonight was our last donated meal. We've got enough leftovers to last us two more nights. After that, I'll add cooking dinner to my already over-busy day. Ingrid leaves at five. We talked about this. You promised me you'd be home by five-fifteen every night once the casseroles ran out. That gives you two more nights." She paused, waiting for his response.

The line remained silent.

"I'm holding you to your promise, Frank. I need you at home. And so do the big kids. They all miss you terribly. You should hear them. They're excited about you being with us in the evenings. Soon, Frank. Soon."

CHAPTER 15

$\mathcal{M}$aggie smiled at Josh as he finished a phone call.

"One of the trustees requested another copy of the agenda for next week's meeting. He thinks he deleted it by mistake." Josh scribbled a note to himself.

"Happens to the best of us," Maggie said. "I'm headed to Rosemont. Gordon Mortimer just texted me; he'll be there in half an hour."

"Sunday's very excited to meet him tomorrow night. So are Lyla and Robert." Josh looked up at Maggie and grinned. "I'm happy to be coming to dinner. I know what a great cook you are."

"Flattering the cook is a surefire way to get invited back." Maggie chuckled. "Would you double-check my calendar? If I don't have any meetings this afternoon, I think I'll work from home the rest of the day."

Josh turned to his computer and tapped the keyboard. "Nope. You're all clear."

"Good. I'd like to be there to settle Gordon in and see if he needs my help in the attic."

"We watched *Antiques Roadshow* every week without fail when I was growing up. I still love it. If I had an attic that might be full of treasures, I'd be beside myself. I'd be right there with him, as he goes through stuff."

"I have to admit, I'm very curious."

"If I see anything important come in, I'll text you. That way you can pay attention to Gordon."

"Thank you, Josh. I'm taking tomorrow off to get ready for the dinner. I'll see you at six."

The phone rang and Josh nodded to her as he picked up the receiver. "President Martin's office," he said, waving her away.

THE MELODIC CHIME of Rosemont's doorbell sounded from the first floor below her.

Roman and Eve sprang to their feet and barked.

Maggie threw on the T-shirt she'd taken out of the closet, zipped her jeans, and raced down the stairs to answer the door.

Roman and Eve followed close at her heels.

"Quiet," she commanded. "Sit."

The dogs obeyed. Roman was the picture of a perfectly

behaved dog; Eve squirmed and whined, but remained in place.

Maggie smoothed her hair and opened Rosemont's massive mahogany front door. "Gordon." She stepped back and motioned for him to come inside.

The tall, balding, middle-aged man stepped inside, rolling his suitcase behind him. He was neatly attired in a button-down shirt, dress slacks, and sport coat. The only concession to the fact that he'd been driving for more than six hours was the loosened silk tie at his neck. "Hello, madam."

"I'm so glad you're here," she said. "You must have made very good time."

"I did. I hope I didn't inconvenience you by being an hour early."

"Not in the least. Come in. Would you like something to drink?"

"If you don't mind, I'd like to change my clothes and get started in the attic."

Maggie couldn't suppress her grin. "I was hoping you'd say that. Let me show you to your room." She started for the staircase.

Eve broke her stay and made a beeline for Gordon.

He bent to pat her as she jumped on his leg.

"Down, Eve," Maggie said. "I'm sorry about that."

"Not at all. I like dogs." Gordon held a hand out to Roman, who remained rooted to his spot. "May I?"

"Okay, Roman. That's a very good boy."

Gordon and Roman exchanged a civilized greeting. "Are the cats…?" His shoulders tensed.

"All three are spending the duration of your visit at Westbury Animal Hospital," Maggie confirmed. "You won't need antihistamines on their account."

"That's very kind of you, madam." He stood, relief evident in his posture.

Maggie led Gordon to the first door on the left at the top of the stairs. "I think you'll be comfortable here," she said. "Your en suite is through there." She pointed to a closed door. "This bedroom has the strongest Wi-Fi signal. I've written the network password on that card on the desk."

"This is a lovely room." He walked to the four-poster bed that dominated the space and examined the carved headboard. When he turned back to her, his eyes were wide. "Have you had the furniture on the first and second floors appraised?"

"Ummm… no. I figured we had some nice antiques, but we never had them appraised."

An exasperated sigh escaped his lips. "I'm certain this bed is a very valuable piece," Gordon said. "I believe I'd better look at more than your attic."

Maggie forcibly suppressed a squeal. "That would be lovely." She stepped to the door. "You get changed and I'll go get us bottles of water."

"Excellent."

"Do you remember where the attic stairs are?"

"I do."

"Then I'll meet you up there," Maggie said, pulling his door shut behind her. She raced down the stairs, dashed off a text to John telling him about Gordon's exciting pronouncement, and went to fetch the promised water bottles.

"THE LIGHT'S FADING." Gordon turned to Maggie. "I think we've made a good start, but it's time to quit."

"Yes. You've had a long day. John will be home soon. He's picking up a couple of shop lights from our friend, Sam Torres. Sam brought his dog in to see John this afternoon and they got to chatting. Sam suggested it."

"Those will be very useful," Gordon said, leading the way to the door at the top of the attic stairs. He turned back. "Thank you for your help. We've sorted furniture to one side, with art and collectibles on the other."

"What about all those boxes of documents and records? Should I trash them?"

Gordon spun on her. "Certainly not, madam." He took a calming breath. "My guess is that you may find valuable items in there, too. Like that stamp we found on my last visit."

"The one that you had me put in our safe."

"I've brought stamp tongs and acid-free tissue. I'd like to take another look at it. I did some research and there are only two other copies in existence."

"So it will be valuable, too?"

"Quite."

"What do we do with it?"

"Stamps, like rare books and coins, are their own specialized collectibles. I recommend we send it off to the philatelic society to have it authenticated."

"That makes sense. How do they do that?"

"Besides a microscopic examination of the surface, they'll test the type of paper, ink, and glue. All of those have to be consistent with what would have been used when the stamp was produced. Stamps aren't signed by the artist like paintings are, so we don't have that element to help us establish authenticity."

"It's all so complicated."

"That's why there are experts in each field."

"And to think these valuable things have been lying around up here—for decades."

Gordon shuddered. "Precisely."

Roman and Eve barked, their voices trailing off toward the kitchen.

"John must be home," Maggie said. "We thought we'd take you to Pete's Bistro for dinner tonight. It's a local favorite, and the food is fabulous."

"That's most kind. If you don't mind, I'd like to move the Thomas Cole downstairs. I've arranged for a white glove transport service to pick it up tomorrow. They'll crate it and send it to be cleaned and restored."

Maggie bit her lip.

"It'll be fully insured—as an original Thomas Cole."

"Good. We have such high hopes for that painting—or rather—the money its sale will raise."

"To fund the service dog school. Such a worthy cause."

"The young man who's about to head to California to

become a guide dog trainer will be at dinner tomorrow night along with his mom. We thought you'd like to meet the person whose dream you're supporting by forgoing your commission."

"I'd like that very much, madam. Thank you."

They turned as footsteps sounded on the stairs behind them. John soon entered the attic, lugging two large shop lights on stands. "I thought I'd find the two of you up here." He leaned the lights against a wall and extended his hand to Gordon.

They shook hands.

"Thank you for bringing those," Maggie said. "They'll be very useful tomorrow. Right now, can you help Gordon carry the Thomas Cole downstairs? Then we'll head out to Pete's."

Gordon and John moved the painting, and they were soon on their way to a relaxing dinner.

CHAPTER 16

*I*ngrid emerged from the laundry room carrying a stack of clean, folded onesies. "Mr. Haynes," she said. "I didn't know you'd be home this afternoon."

Frank eased the door into the garage shut behind him. "I was driving by on my way back to the office and wanted to…" he trailed off, as if he didn't know why he was there.

"See your babies?" Ingrid gestured to the family room. "They're in there. They've just been fed and Loretta's rocking them."

"Will I be interrupting?"

"Of course not. Loretta will be delighted to see you." She gave him an encouraging smile. "You work so hard, all the time. You deserve a quiet moment with your wife and those babies." She continued down the hall to the nursery.

Frank walked to the family room and stopped abruptly in the entryway. Loretta was slouched down on the sofa with her feet propped on an ottoman. She cradled Branson in one arm and Bonnie in the other. All three of them had their eyes closed.

He stood, observing the peaceful scene in front of him. Their chests rose and fell in sleep. Branson pushed one tiny arm out of his blanket and stretched it across Loretta's chest toward his sister. As if by instinct, Bonnie extricated her arm and reached for him. Their hands met and clasped.

Frank's breath caught in his throat.

Loretta stirred and opened her eyes. They grew wide when she saw Frank in the doorway.

He put his finger to his lips.

She glanced at the clasped hands on her chest and grinned. "They do that all the time, now," she whispered. "Every time they're close enough to touch."

Frank blinked away tears.

"Come join us," Loretta said.

Frank crossed to a chair next to the sofa.

"No. Sit with us on the sofa."

"I don't want to disturb them."

"You won't." She beckoned to him with her eyes.

Frank lowered himself slowly next to her.

Branson and Bonnie kept sleeping.

"I'm glad to see you," Loretta said.

"I told Ingrid I was stopping by on my way back to the office, but that's a lie."

Loretta raised her brows.

"I was at my desk, working away, and I just *had* to leave. I needed to come home to you and these guys." He moved a tendril of hair out of her eyes.

"I'm glad you did," Loretta said. "They're the sweetest things in the whole wide world. By the time you get home, you're beat from working like a maniac all day and I'm exhausted. It's not the ideal situation to appreciate each other."

Frank exhaled softly. "Looking at the three of you, just now... well... I cannot believe how lucky I am."

"You weren't thinking 'what a frumpy woman I'm married to'?" Loretta tugged at the T-shirt and joggers she'd worn for the past three days.

"Are you kidding me?" He drew back and placed his palm on her cheek. "You're even more beautiful now than the first day I met you." He leaned in and kissed her.

"I'm thrilled to hear that," she said, squirming in her seat. "I've got a favor to ask."

"Anything."

"Would you hold them for me? I've got to go to the bathroom." She leaned toward him and slid the babies into his open arms.

Frank held his breath. Branson and Bonnie slept on, their hands together. He settled against the back of the sofa.

Loretta sped out of the room. When she returned, moments later, it was her turn to pause in the doorway.

Frank was sitting, head down, with one baby in each arm nestled against his neck.

She tiptoed to him. "There's nothing like holding your sleeping child."

97

He nodded his agreement.

Loretta eased into place next to him. "Come home anytime, Frank. Whenever you feel like it. You are the big boss, you know. The one whose name is on the door? Moments like these are precious—you don't want to miss them."

"I'd like to. I'll try."

His cell phone began to ring.

He bit off the curse that sprang to his lips. "Here," he said, holding the sleeping infants out to her.

Loretta scooped them up.

Frank answered the call and listened. "Tell them I got detained at one of the restaurants and I'll be there in ten minutes." He continued to listen. "Yes. Offer them coffee. See you soon."

Loretta cocked her head to one side. "Do you have to leave?"

"I'm afraid so. Our divisional manager from franchise headquarters is here for our semi-annual meeting. It's been on the books for months. I completely forgot." He bent and kissed her. "I'm sorry."

"Don't worry. We're here whenever you can sneak away."

"I'd better not keep this guy waiting."

"Maybe you should change your shirt before meeting with Mr. Important." She smiled at him. "You've got something crusty on each shoulder—like you've been holding babies."

Frank ran his hands over the offending spots. "Good call. Thanks." He hurried to their bedroom and changed his shirt before retying his tie. He moved toward the door, then went back to the mirror.

Frank untied and retied his necktie two more times before forcing himself to step away from the mirror and head to his office.

CHAPTER 17

*M*aggie returned to the dining room and stood behind her chair at one end of the table. The easy flow of conversation among her guests stopped as all eyes turned to her.

"It's a perfect spring evening. Let's have dessert and coffee on the back patio. You've got your choice of chocolate cake or peach pie from Laura's."

"Or both," John interjected from the other end of the table.

"Absolutely," Maggie agreed. "Help yourself to pie or cake —or both," she winked at her husband, "on your way through the kitchen. Coffee is set up outside."

Chairs scraped against the wood floor as the dinner guests stood, laid their antique embroidered napkins on the linen tablecloth, and made their way to the kitchen island where dessert was displayed on tiered silver stands.

David hung back, and Gordon stayed with him. "I'm impressed by your commitment to open a service dog training school here. Not many high school seniors have such a definite idea of what they want to do with their lives."

David shrugged. "I learned, firsthand, the life-changing impact dogs can make on people's lives when Dodger and I started working as a therapy dog team. I'd never had a dog before and I was amazed."

"John told me about your remarkable facility with dogs. He says you're intuitive."

A swath of crimson crept from David's collar to the top of his head.

"How did you start working with Dodger as a therapy team?"

David took a deep breath and turned his face to the floor. "It was part of my community service."

Gordon didn't speak.

David looked up at him. The expression in the prim and proper man's eyes was kind and encouraging.

"I got into trouble after my dad went to prison. I took some stuff from school. I didn't even want it—I don't know why I did it." He shook his head. "Maybe to get attention. I don't know. Anyway—I got caught. The court assigned Glenn Vaughn to be my mentor, and he got me an internship at Forever Friends. That's the no-kill animal shelter that Frank Haynes founded. Frank and Glenn convinced my mom to let me get a dog. I adopted Dodger, and we became a therapy dog team. I decided right away that I wanted to spend my life training dogs to help people."

Gordon put his hand on David's shoulder. "That's admirable. We all make mistakes. Successful people learn from them and choose a different path moving forward."

"Thank you."

"Tell me about this apprenticeship program you're about to enter."

"I'll be a kennel assistant at the Guide Dog Center for about six months—until they have an opening in the training program. I'll get to know the people and their operation while I'm assisting in the kennels. They'll see how I work with the puppies, too. If I'm a good fit..."

"I'm sure you will be," Gordon interjected.

"I'll start apprenticing to become a seeing eye dog trainer."

"How long does this training take?"

"Two to three years. They encourage apprentices to take college classes while they're in the program, so that might cause delays."

"Will you do that? Get your degree?"

David nodded. "I plan—one day, down the road—to become a veterinarian."

A smile spread across Gordon's habitually serious face. "That's a terrific idea, David. You've set yourself some worthy goals."

"The Guide Dog Center has a team of specialized vets who oversee their in-house breeding program and deter-mine if a dog has the physical hardiness to be a guide—in addition to providing regular medical care to the dogs in their program. If I'm going to start a school here, I think it'll be good for me to be a veterinarian. John says he'll donate his time to be the school's vet until I get out of school."

"You've really thought this out. What are your plans for the school?"

"I'll open it as a sister company to Forever Friends. We'll call it Forever Guides. There's a vacant lot next to Forever Friends. Frank says it's big enough for the school. We'll need money to build and staff the school."

"How much does a seeing eye dog cost?"

"Nothing. I want anyone who needs a dog to get one for free. Medical care for the life of the dog will be provided without charge, too. The only thing the owner should pay for is food and toys."

Gordon swallowed the growing lump in his throat. "As I said before, I'm very impressed with you, David. I'm happy to forgo my commission on the Van Cleef & Arpels brooch being auctioned next month, the Thomas Cole painting we're sending out for refurbishment prior to auction, and anything else Maggie donates to the cause."

"Thank you so much." David stuck his hand out awkwardly toward the adult man.

Gordon shook it warmly. "I'm proud to be a small part of your dream."

Judy Young rounded the corner on them. "There you are." She fixed her gaze on Gordon. "All that talk during dinner about rare books and designer jewelry reminded me of something else."

"Oh?" Gordon released David's hand, and the boy slipped away to snag his dessert.

"One of my friends has a basement full of vintage sewing machines."

"Those are collectible," Gordon said. "Some are quite valuable. How did she come into their possession?"

"Anita owns the local bridal shop. She inherited it from her mother. Archer's Bridal has been in her family for three generations. They're machines that were used in the shop. Some of them are very worn, but a few really old ones are in fabulous shape. They've got gold-plated lettering and every-thing—they're really quite beautiful."

"She may have some nice pieces."

"She's talked for years about getting rid of them—she just doesn't know how. Would you look at them when you come back to go through the Olsson house attic?"

"I'd be delighted to, madam."

Judy clasped her hands together. "I can't wait to tell Anita. She'll be thrilled." She stepped back and tilted her head to one side. "You haven't had dessert yet, have you?"

Gordon shook his head.

"We've all been talking your ear off since we sat down to dinner. You're going to think that people from Westbury have no manners." She took his elbow and steered him to the kitchen island. "There's one remaining slice of each of the cake and the pie. I'd snag both of them if I were you."

Gordon protested.

"I'm serious. Laura's is the best bakery in the state. Go on." She picked up a fork and slid the slice of cake onto the plate with the pie, handing it to him. "Everyone else has had theirs. Now come outside with me."

Gordon followed Judy with a spring in his step. It wasn't often he got to spend an evening with people who were passionate about the things he devoted his life to.

Sunday and Robert intercepted them as Judy and Gordon stepped onto the patio.

"We were coming to find you," Sunday said.

"I just realized I'll be in London on business when the auction of the brooch takes place," Robert said.

"Would you like to attend? I'll be there. I'd be happy to bring you as my guest," Gordon replied.

"That would be terrific. I've been to rare-book auctions, but not ones for other items. I've always wanted to go."

Gordon pulled out his phone. "Let's share contact information. I'll forward all the details to you later tonight."

"That's very kind of you, Gordon," Robert said. "I'm still liquidating the inventory of Blythe Rare Books. The purpose of my trip is to pack up and move the remaining volumes from the storefront so the estate can vacate the premises. Would you like to see what's there while you're in London? I'd like you to pick out a volume for your collection, as a thank-you for getting me into an auction like this."

"That's extremely generous of you, Robert. But not necessary."

"I insist," Robert said. "I'll reply to your email with the address of Blythe Rare Books. You can drop by whenever's convenient for you."

The two men nodded at each other, happy to have made a friend with a shared interest.

CHAPTER 18

"Frank," Loretta blew out a breath when he answered his cell phone. "I didn't think I was going to get you. Will you pick up a gallon of milk on the way home? We're out."

"I just bought two gallons yesterday evening."

"I know. We ran through one for breakfast and dinner. We opened the second one for hot chocolate after the kids finished their homework and Nicole pushed it off the counter. It spilled all over, everywhere. And now we don't have any for breakfast."

"What the hell? I'll talk to her about being more careful."

"You'll do no such thing. It was an accident, Frank. She felt terrible about it. Cried and cried. Just stop and pick up another gallon—make it two. You are on your way home, aren't you?"

Frank didn't answer.

"Frank! You promised you'd be home for dinner every night once I was cooking again. That was a week ago and you haven't made it once."

"Yes. I'm on my way," Frank lied.

"You could have said so," Loretta quipped. "So you'll pick up milk?"

"Yes." His voice was hard. "Anything else?"

"May as well get a loaf of bread. And a bag of apples. And some string cheese. Plus, we're almost out of peanut butter."

Frank ground his teeth together.

"You got all that?"

"Yes, Loretta."

The sound of a crying baby emanated from Loretta's side of the call. "I've gotta go. See you soon. And thank you."

Frank grunted his acknowledgment and swiped to end the call. He looked at the time on his phone. He'd be three hours later getting home than he'd promised her. And it would still be the earliest he'd come home from work since the babies had been born.

He pressed his hands to his temples. What in the world was wrong with him? He loved all five of his children and he adored his wife even more than before she'd given birth. Why was he so irritable and rude? It was like he couldn't control his mouth.

He stood abruptly, knocking his tiered metal inbox to the floor. He told himself he should leave it until the morning. Running by the grocery store would make him even later getting home. He didn't need to add any additional delay to his departure.

Frank bent over and picked up the inbox. He set it on his desk and repositioned it several times. Taking a ruler from his lap drawer, he made sure the inbox was equidistant from the edge of the desk at both ends. He then painstakingly returned each piece of paper to the appropriate tray.

He picked up the ruler and brought it to the lap drawer, but didn't put it back into its place. Instead, he verified the placement of the inbox five more times, moving one end or the other an infinitesimal amount.

His hand shook the last time. Frank knew he needed to stop. He shoved the ruler into the drawer and slammed it shut. He picked up his car keys and strode swiftly out the door. Frank inserted his key into the lock from the outside and turned it from locked to unlocked repeatedly while he counted to ten, pulling on the handle to verify the door was locked before starting the process over again.

He forced himself to turn his back on the door and walk to his car, knowing he had to get out of there. He had to stop at the store and go home. The family he loved needed him.

FRANK SET the grocery bags on the counter. The kitchen was dark, illuminated only by light spilling over from the hallway to the bedrooms.

He knelt to pat Sally, his faithful border collie mix, who circled at his feet, waiting for his attention. "Where are your buddies—Snowball and Daisy?" he asked.

"They sleep with Nicole and Sean," Loretta replied quietly. "They're already in bed."

Frank startled. "I didn't see you there."

"Was the grocery busy at this time of night, Frank? I expected you an hour ago."

Frank got to his feet and began to unload the groceries. He took a large mixed bouquet, wrapped in cellophane, and handed it to her. "These are colors you like. I wanted you to have them."

Loretta took the flowers from him.

"I'm sorry I was late."

"These are lovely, Frank. Thank you. Can you get a vase out of the cabinet above the refrigerator?"

Frank retrieved the vase and set it on the counter. He picked up the jar of peanut butter.

"I can put the groceries away," Loretta said, filling the vase with water. "Sean's been waiting up for you. Go spend time with him."

Frank turned his face to the floor, then nodded.

"He needs you. We all do."

Frank swung to her, anger in his eyes.

Loretta put up a hand. "Let's not do this now. Go see Sean. It'll be time to feed Bonnie and Branson in another half hour. We can talk then."

Frank nodded and walked down the hall to Sean's bedroom. He knocked softly before turning the knob and entering the room.

"Dad!" Sean said in a voice that was half sleepy and half excited.

"Hey, buddy." Frank sat at the foot of the bed.

Daisy lay curled up next to Sean. She thumped her tail on the bed.

Frank stroked her silky fur.

"How are you, son?"

"Great. Have you talked to David? About Forever Friends?"

"No. I've been buried at work. I haven't been by there in weeks."

Sean propped himself up on his elbows. "He's been training me—ever since the twins were born."

"Oh?"

"Yeah. To take over for him when he goes to California."

"I remember now. You're a lot younger than he is, Sean. I don't know…"

"I'm the same age he was when he started at Forever Friends. David told me. He also said I'm great with all the animals," Sean said in a rush. "He thinks I can do it."

Frank looked into the earnest eyes of this boy he loved. "We don't have to decide right now."

Sean sighed heavily.

"I promise we'll talk about it."

"Okay. We never see you anymore, so I—"

"I'm doing the best I can, son." Frank cut him off. "Providing for this family is my responsibility. Running Haynes Enterprises takes a lot of time." His tone was sharp.

Sean recoiled at the rebuke.

Frank leapt to his feet. "It's late and you've got school tomorrow. You need to get to sleep."

"Don't be mad at me, Dad." Sean's voice was contrite.

Frank rubbed his hand across the back of his neck. "I'm sorry. I'm not mad." He kissed the top of the boy's head. "I'll come see you in action at Forever Friends next week—or the week after, at the latest."

Sean snuggled into his pillow. "That'd be great, Dad."

Frank turned out the overhead light in Sean's room and closed the door behind him as he entered the hall. The sounds of whimpering that he identified as Branson's reached his paternal ears. Frank headed toward the nursery.

Loretta was already picking up Bonnie. "Right on cue," she smiled at Frank. "Did you have a good chat with Sean?"

Frank nodded. He knew that he and Loretta should discuss Sean's desire to work at Forever Friends, but he was exhausted. All he wanted to do was get the twins fed and crawl into bed.

"I made a plate for you and put it in the oven to warm up. Meatloaf and mashed potatoes—your favorite. Help me get these two situated for nursing and then go get your supper. You can bring it in here and we can talk while they nurse." Loretta sat in the oversize rocking chair.

Frank helped her position the babies. "Thank you, but I'm not hungry."

Loretta lifted her eyes to his. "Have you eaten anything today?"

Frank shrugged.

"You're shedding weight faster than I am. In my case, that's a good thing. I want to lose my baby weight. That's not the case with you. Aren't you hungry?"

"I don't have much of an appetite these days."

"That's not healthy, Frank. I'm worried about you."

"Don't be. I'm fine. You've got enough on your hands with the kids."

"That's exactly why I need adult conversation about something other than them. I'm trapped in this house all day, every day. I'm accustomed to being with you during the day at Haynes Enterprises."

Frank stood motionless in the doorway.

"Don't you want to be with us anymore, Frank? Have I... aren't you attracted to me anymore?"

"It's not that. Of course I want to be with all of you. And you're still the most beautiful, wonderful, desirable woman in the world. That hasn't changed."

"Then what is it?"

"Revenues have been uneven. I've got a family of seven to support now. That means five kids who may need braces—and money for dance classes and sports—and who will eventually need college educations. It's all on me now. I'm working hard to make sure we can afford all those things."

"Surely it's not as dire as all that. You've been extremely successful. By all standards, we're rich."

Frank swung on her. "Are you saying you don't believe me?" His voice rose an octave.

"Keep your voice down. We don't want to wake the kids. I'm not accusing you of anything." Her voice broke. "I just miss you, that's all."

"You keep saying that! I get it," he hissed.

A silent tear slid down Loretta's cheek. "I don't want to fight."

Frank's shoulders drooped. He walked to the rocking chair and dropped to one knee. "Sweetheart, I'm sorry. I miss all of you, too. I'm just trying to do my best."

Loretta leaned toward him and rested her forehead against his. "I can make do without Ingrid, if that will help."

"No! You need—and deserve—her help. Things aren't that bad. I'm just worrying long term."

"I'll stop bugging you to be home for dinner."

"Thank you. I may have to work late for quite a while yet. You and the kids can order out dinner every night. Would it help if you didn't have to cook?"

Loretta considered this. "I look forward to cooking dinner. It's relaxing. I know this sounds crazy, but it's creative too. I want to continue making dinner."

"Okay, but if it ever gets to be too much, you can always have meals delivered."

Bonnie finished nursing and Frank burped her and changed her diaper in record time.

"Look at you," Loretta said. "You could be in the Guinness Book," she teased.

Frank grinned for the first time since he'd been home. "I have gotten good, haven't I?"

"And how!" Loretta stood and walked to the changing table. "I'm not that efficient. You're as good as Ingrid."

"Now that's really saying something. With all her years working as a nurse in a hospital nursery, she must be lightning fast." Frank laid a satisfied Branson in his bassinet.

"I'll take care of Bonnie," Loretta said. "I want you to go to the kitchen and eat that meatloaf that's waiting for you in the oven."

Frank leaned in and kissed her temple. He went to the kitchen and removed the plate from the oven. He tore back the foil. Steam poured off a generous portion of the meal he loved. He brought the plate to his nose and sniffed. It smelled good.

Frank stood over the plate at the counter and skewered a forkful of meat and potatoes. His stomach lurched when he brought it to his lips. He opened his mouth, but the food held no appeal for him. He couldn't force himself to eat.

Frank picked up the plate and slid the contents into the sink. He ran the garbage disposal, rinsed his plate, and loaded it into the dishwasher.

He padded down the hall to his bedroom. Loretta was already in bed and her deep breathing told him she was asleep. He settled into bed next to her, hoping it wouldn't take him until the wee hours to get to sleep.

CHAPTER 19

*M*aggie looked across the street to the town square from her table for two in the front window of Pete's Bistro. Even though she and John had just dined there with Gordon, she was happy to be in its welcoming environment again. The personal attention the bistro provided all its patrons was one reason it had been named top restaurant in Westbury for each of the past ten years. Pete always sat her at this table in the window when she was waiting for Susan. Maggie loved seeing the busy after-work hubbub while she watched for Susan to arrive for their monthly mother-daughter dinner.

Employees poured out of Town Hall on the other side of the square, headed for the parking garage or the bus stop. She knew many of them from her tenure as mayor. It seemed like a lifetime ago.

A full-size white SUV drove by slowly. Maggie recognized her daughter at the wheel. The car came to a stop and Susan skillfully maneuvered the behemoth into a parking spot at the curb. Maggie shook her head. How her daughter had learned to parallel park with the skill of a stunt driver, she'd never know.

The door to Pete's swung open and Susan stepped inside. Tall and trim, she cut an elegant figure in her tailored suit, heels, and crisp white button-down.

Susan headed directly to the table, where she knew her mother would be waiting.

Maggie rose and the two women threw their arms around each other in a tight hug.

"I'm glad we do that," Susan said, releasing her mother. "Hug like we mean it. I hope Julia and I will do it, too."

"I'm sure you will." Maggie sat, warmed by her daughter's comment. An adult child's desire to continue habits and traditions with their children brought a special happiness.

Pete walked up to their table, holding out menus. "Would you ladies like to see menus?"

Both women shook their heads no in unison.

"Is the special still rainbow trout, fingerling potatoes, and green beans?" Maggie asked.

Pete nodded. "I tried to change up the nightly specials several years ago and was almost ridden out of town on a rail. People around here aren't looking for the latest and greatest—at least not from my restaurant."

"Rightly so," Susan said. "I deal with change all day long at my job. I don't want it at my favorite dinner spot. I'm happy with choices I can count on."

"That being said," Pete looked between them, "shall I put in your order for two trout specials, iced teas, and pieces of the pie of the day?"

"Yes." Again, they answered in unison.

"So," Susan leaned across the table to Maggie as Pete walked away. "How did it go with Gordon?"

"Fabulous," Maggie said. "He had the Cole sent off for cleaning and found at least six pieces of furniture in the attic that he believes we should put up for sale at a luxury auction house. They're all eighteenth-century English pieces."

"That's so exciting. Anything else?"

"He also thinks the four-poster bed in the guest room on the left at the top of the stairs is valuable. Actually, he called it a priceless antique."

"Are you going to sell it, too?"

"I haven't decided yet. I love the piece and it looks perfect in the room."

"You could easily buy another bed frame that would look wonderful there," Susan said.

"I know. I think I'll wait to see how much money we raise from the sale of the furniture in the attic. Right now, I don't need to do anything."

"No. Of course not."

"Gordon also sent the stamp to a philatelic society for authentication."

"He's knowledgeable about a wide range of things."

"That he is. You should have heard him at dinner, talking to Robert and Sunday about rare books. He knew as much as they did."

"How did the dinner go?"

"I think it was a terrific success. I certainly learned a lot. Gordon and Robert have been going back and forth about Robert's upcoming trip to England. Gordon has invited him to attend the auction where my Van Cleef & Arpels brooch will be sold. Josh told me they've become fast friends."

"I love hearing that."

"Me too," Maggie said. "I know, firsthand, how daunting it can be to move to a new city—let alone a new country—like Robert did. Even though he had Lyla and Josh, everything familiar changed for him."

"I've always admired that you had the courage to move here after Dad's sudden death."

Maggie raised her eyebrows at Susan.

Pete brought their iced teas to the table.

"I know I may not have been supportive of the move—at first," Susan conceded. "It was such a shock for both Mike and me."

"And look how it turned out for all of us. Eve adopted me, which led me to John."

"Your working with Alex resulted in my meeting—and marrying—his brother. Let's face it, if you hadn't moved to Rosemont, you wouldn't have met John, I wouldn't be with Aaron, and Julia would never have been born."

Pete set their entrees on the table. He knew enough not to interrupt their conversation and moved away after smiling at them.

"It seemed crazy at the time—even to me—to move across the country and into the abandoned mansion that I never knew your father had inherited. But it's brought so much joy to me and everyone around me. I've said it before—there's magic in that house."

"You really believe that, don't you?"

"Absolutely. Look at all the valuables we've found in the attic. I think about all the good things we'll do with the money we raise from their sale and about all the people we've met because of Rosemont."

"I can't argue with that." Susan took a bite of potato. "Who knows—maybe Rosemont has more tricks up her sleeve."

Maggie set her fork and knife on the rim of her plate and lowered her head slightly as she leaned toward her daughter.

Susan looked at her mother. "Your eyes are twinkling. Something's up, isn't it?" Her tone was gleeful. "Tell me," she practically squealed.

"I didn't mention it, but I think Gordon had a wonderful time when he was here."

Susan sank back into her chair. "I'm sure he did, but so what? He lives in New York, doesn't he?"

"He does, but he mentioned to me how delightful he thinks Westbury is. He even drove around town, exploring. When he got back to Rosemont, he was full of information about the historic district around the square. He'd been researching online." Maggie voiced the last statement like a vindication of her point.

"He's interested in old things for his job, Mom. He does research for that all the time. It's just how he rolls." She turned her attention back to her meal. "I'm sure it doesn't mean anything."

Maggie continued, her enthusiasm unabated. "That's not all. As we were just saying, he's made a fast friend in Robert. I sense he doesn't have good friends in New York."

Susan rolled her eyes. "Then they'll email, text, and call each other."

"Judy is going to introduce him to Anita Archer," Maggie said in a rush. She patted her lips with her napkin and sat back in her chair, as if this changed everything.

Susan chortled. "Do you think… are you saying… that Gordon and Anita would hit it off? You can't be serious."

Maggie's brows drew together. "I most certainly am. You haven't met Gordon, but you know Anita. She's a lovely woman."

"I agree."

"They both study and appreciate beautiful things. Anita has an encyclopedic knowledge of twentieth-century courtier clothing."

"That's true. Is Gordon interested in clothes?"

"I don't know—but that's not the point. They're both connoisseurs. There's a certain mindset—a sensibility—that goes along with that."

"You're saying they're the same sort of person?" Susan asked.

"Exactly."

"It's still an enormous leap to being a love match." Susan sipped her tea.

"Judy agrees with me. In fact, it was her idea in the first place."

Susan chuckled. "With you and Judy on the case, Gordon doesn't stand a chance."

Maggie nodded. "Promise me you won't say anything to Aaron."

"Because you haven't mentioned this matchmaking scheme to John. You don't want Aaron to spill the beans. Am I right?"

"You know John teases me about wanting everyone around me to be in love."

Susan reached for her mother's hand and squeezed it. "It's one of your most endearing qualities. You're committed to love."

Maggie patted Susan's hand. "You'll keep this little secret to yourself?"

Susan nodded. "Of course I will. If there's anything I can do to help, count me in. If Anita and Gordon are meant to be together, let's make it happen."

The two women were grinning at each other when Pete brought them dessert.

CHAPTER 20

"Susan!" Nicole cried as she opened the door to her half-sister. The bond the two shared after Susan had donated a life-saving kidney to Nicole was undeniable. Nicole flung her arms around Susan's waist.

Susan stooped to hug Nicole tightly. "Hey, sweetie. How's my girl?"

Nicole tilted her head to look at Susan.

Susan brushed Nicole's hair off of her forehead and planted a kiss in the center.

"I'm good. Are you here to see the babies?"

"And your mom, if she's around. I'm dropping something off for her." Susan picked up the heavy canvas bag she'd set at her feet when she'd greeted Nicole. "I texted her that I'd stop by on my way home from work."

"She's in the kitchen, making dinner." Nicole moved back

so Susan could step inside. "She's in a grouchy mood," Nicole whispered.

"Your mom's got a lot on her plate right now."

Nicole furrowed her brows. "She's not done cooking. There's nothing on any plates."

Susan chuckled. "That's an expression. It means she has a lot going on. I'm sure she's tired and overwhelmed."

Nicole nodded sagely. "The babies are a lot. That's what she just told Frank on the phone. I overheard."

Susan rubbed her sister's back. "This will all get better. It takes time."

Loretta popped her head out of the kitchen. "I thought I heard the door." She wore pajama pants and a T-shirt. A terry-cloth robe hung open from her shoulders. She tucked a hank of her long blonde hair that had escaped her ponytail behind an ear.

Susan walked toward her, lugging the canvas bag. "I brought my electric breast pump," she said. "Where would you like it?"

"You can put it," Loretta looked around her, then threw up her hands, "anywhere."

"Let's place this where you plan to pump. I'll help you set it up and go over how to use it. The directions are in the bag for reference, but this way you won't have to waste time with them."

"That's a good idea. I'll use it in our bedroom. Hang on a minute." Loretta stepped back into the kitchen and turned down a burner as a pot of spaghetti was about to boil over.

"Do you need a hand with dinner?" Susan asked, looking at the mess of empty boxes, wrappers, and jars strewn across the counters.

"No. I browned hamburger, boiled noodles, and opened a bag of mixed greens. All I need to do now is microwave a jar of spaghetti sauce. That's as good as it gets for a home cooked-meal these days."

"It sounds wonderful," Susan said. "We have that meal at my house, too."

"You're not always whipping up the latest recipe from the *New York Times?*"

Susan snorted. "I'm afraid not. I used to be a pretty good cook, but that went out the window when Julia came along. I simply don't have the time."

Loretta stood straighter. "Follow me." She led the way to the bedroom. "This is really nice of you to let me try your pump. It's expensive and… well… I don't want to waste our money on something I won't use."

"It was a lifesaver for me. You can keep it as long as you like. I don't need it anymore. Don't bother buying one. Just return it whenever you're done with it."

"That's kind of you." Loretta flipped on the overhead light switch. "I've got a small desk against the wall. I thought I'd pump while I'm on the computer or reading a magazine."

"That'll be perfect. Multi-tasking is the name of the game for mothers." Susan began unpacking the pump.

"The outlet is on the wall, underneath the desk." Loretta pointed to it.

The two women worked together and Susan explained how to use and care for the helpful piece of equipment.

"That seems easy," Loretta said.

"You won't have any problem with it—and if you do, just call me." Susan looked toward the hallway. "Are they up? I'd love to see them."

Loretta shook her head. "I fed them and put them down right before you got here. Ingrid helps me with them before she leaves for the day. That's supposed to give me time to make dinner."

"That makes sense. Are Branson and Bonnie getting on a schedule?"

"They are during the day, when Ingrid's here. She's fabulous. Everything goes smoothly. Evenings—when I'm on my own with all five of the kids—are chaos. Dinner, dishes, homework, baths, bedtime—it's a nightmare."

Susan cocked her head to one side. "Where's Frank?"

Loretta shook her head slowly. "He's never here. He says things aren't going well with the business and—now that we have two more mouths to feed—he works eighteen hours a day."

"Sounds like my life, being married to an orthopedic surgeon who's low man on the totem pole at his practice. He was on call constantly. I thought I was going to lose my mind —and I only had one child."

"How'd you get through it?"

"I had a nanny—like you do—but I also hired a mother's helper for the evening hours. Actually—you might know her:

Grace Acosta. She was a high school junior and was wonderful."

"I've never met her."

Susan snapped her fingers. "That's it. You should hire Grace. She just graduated and is going to Highpointe in the fall. Her dad's a professor there. Anyway—I ran into her at Laura's last week. She's working part time in the morning and is looking for another job. She wants to save as much money as she can before she starts college."

Loretta's eyes grew hopeful. "Do you think she'd be interested in helping... here?"

"I'm sure she would. She's great with babies—and older children, too." Susan squeezed Loretta's elbow. "This is the answer for you."

"Will you introduce us?"

Susan pulled her phone from the pocket of her slacks. "I'll send you both a text right now." She tapped at the screen and pushed send. The phone emitted the telltale swooshing sound.

Loretta and Susan smiled at each other.

"There's one more thing I think you need," Susan said as Loretta walked her to the front door.

"What's that?"

"You need to get out of the house." Her eyes traveled the length of Loretta's disheveled appearance.

"I've been out to take the babies to their doctor's appointments. And I've had my postnatal checkup."

"I mean, without the kids and not to a medical appointment. Or even the grocery store. I'm talking about something fun and social for yourself. You need time with your friends."

Loretta looked away from Susan. Her shoulders sagged.

"You're joining a book club," Susan pronounced. "It saved my sanity when Julia was small and I still look forward to it every month."

"I don't have time to read a book every month," Loretta replied.

"I don't, either. The only ones who read the book every single month are Lyla and Sunday—you'd expect that, since they're librarians—and my mom. She's always been a voracious reader. The rest of us—that's Joan, Judy, Anita, and Tonya—may try to read the book, but we come to book club for the camaraderie and conversation. You know all these gals."

Loretta nodded in agreement.

"It's settled. The next meeting is a week from Wednesday. At my house, 6:30. You're coming."

Loretta lifted her eyes to Susan's. "Okay. I guess I could try it. Out of curiosity—what's the book?"

Susan put her hand to her head. "I'm embarrassed to say this, but I don't remember. It's sitting on my nightstand and I haven't opened it. My mom's finished it. I'll ask her to drop her copy off for you."

"That'd be very nice. I can't believe how kind everyone has been to me." Loretta's voice cracked. "Especially with my history…"

"That's all in the past." Susan pulled her into a hug. "We

all love you, Loretta. We're your friends and we're here for you."

"Mom—when do we eat?" Sean hollered as he came in the back door with Daisy.

Susan stepped back. "I'm going to be on my way and let you finish making dinner. See you next week."

Loretta tightened the sash on her robe and smoothed her hair. "Thank you, Susan. I feel better already."

CHAPTER 21

"Go on," Grace said to Marissa. "Your mom's in the kitchen, starting dinner. Talk to her."

Grace perched at the foot of Marissa's bed. She pulled her long, strawberry blonde hair into a high ponytail and slipped an elastic hair tie from her wrist to secure it. "Your mom wants you to continue with your activities."

Marissa shrugged. "I think she needs me here."

"Maybe before, but I'm here now. I'll come every weekday afternoon and I can help on weekends, too."

"I lied to Mom when I told her that our troupe leader quit and we weren't dancing anymore. She'll be mad at me."

"That was a white lie. Your intentions were good. You wanted to be home to help your family. It's different from a mean-spirited, selfish lie. She'll understand."

"You think so?"

"Absolutely." Grace looked the younger girl in the eyes. "My little brother, Tommy, had eye surgery when I was about your age. I dropped out of the drama program at school to help at home. When my mom found out, she was heartbroken. She said she'd let me down by paying so much attention to Tommy."

"My mom loved to come to our recitals. She signed me up for any lessons I wanted—even when we didn't have much money—before she married Frank."

"I'm sure she still feels the same way. Don't give up something you love—and are good at. Loretta's going to find out sometime and she'll hate that you didn't talk to her about it."

"I think so, too." Marissa and Grace didn't notice the diminutive figure standing in the doorway, listening to their conversation. "Mom wants you to dance," Nicole said. "I heard her tell Frank that they need to find you a new dance school."

"You see?" Grace asked.

Marissa nodded, a smile spreading across her face. "Okay. I'll go talk to her."

"When do you have to be there?"

"6:30," Marissa said.

"I can stay here with this gal," Grace walked to the doorway and ruffled Nicole's hair, "and the babies, or drive you to dance. Whatever your mom wants."

Marissa scooted past Grace and Nicole and headed toward the kitchen.

Nicole turned to follow her sister.

Grace put a hand on the little girl's shoulder. "Marissa and your mom can discuss this between themselves."

Nicole set her face in a pout.

"I haven't seen your room yet," Grace said. "I hear you have a ton of stuffed animals. I have a big collection, too. Will you show them to me?"

"Sure!" Nicole's eyes lit up. "I've got them in a hammock over my bed." Nicole led the way to her room.

They climbed onto the bed. Nicole picked up the lone animal—a rabbit—that reclined against her pillow. His enormous ears flopped over a face that was missing one eye. The plush fur was worn into shiny bare spots on his belly and shoulders. "This is Princess Lolly," Nicole said. "You can call her Lolly."

"What a perfect name for her. She looks like a princess." Grace extended a hand toward the toy.

Nicole pulled back, hugging Lolly to herself. "She's shy around other people."

"Okay. I understand. Can you tell me about her?"

"She's my favorite. Frank gave her to me when I was sick in the hospital—before Susan gave me one of her kidneys. I got better after that."

"I heard. It's wonderful to have a friend with you when you're going through something scary."

"That's why she sleeps with me on the bed. She's afraid to be up there," she pointed to the hammock above their heads, "with the others."

"That's very considerate of you to keep her near you," Grace said.

"I love all the rest of them, too," Nicole said. She replaced Princess Lolly on her pillow. "I'm going to show Grace the others," she told Lolly matter-of-factly. "It's like Mom says about Branson and Bonnie—just because she loves them, it doesn't mean she loves the rest of us any less." She stood on the bed and began removing stuffed animals from the hammock. They were soon surrounded by a mound of stuffed bears, dogs, cats, unicorns, frogs, and more. Grace listened to Nicole with rapt attention as she relayed where, when, and how she'd acquired each one.

They were halfway through the pile when Marissa burst into the room, smiling ear to ear. "You were right! She said she feels terribly guilty that I quit dance to help with the babies."

"I thought she'd say that."

"Mom says that we're still kids and that she and Frank are the parents. This goes for you, too, Nicole. And for Sean. They appreciate our help, but we're not supposed to act like parents. That's their job. Ours is to continue to do our own things. She said she may be distracted for a while, so we should tell her if we need something and they don't notice."

Nicole nodded solemnly. "We can do that."

"Did she say if she wants me to drive you?"

"She said that would be great. Dinner will be ready in fifteen minutes. We can eat and then leave."

"That works."

"I'm going to change and make sure I've got my dance shoes in my bag," Marissa said.

"We won't be done with my animals by then."

"We can finish when I get back from dropping Marissa off. I can help you put them all back." She pointed to the empty hammock over their heads. "And I can read you a bedtime story. How does that sound?"

"Great!" Nicole bounced onto her knees and picked up a stuffed giraffe. "This one came from a famous toy store," she said, launching into her recitation.

SEAN ENTERED the kitchen as Loretta pulled a loaf of bread from the freezer. Daisy and Snowball trailed behind him. He unclipped their leashes. Snowball joined Sally in an oversize memory foam dog bed in the corner. Daisy remained at his side.

"Did you have a good walk?"

Sean nodded. "Snowball's finally stopped pulling on the leash. I think she's learning from Daisy."

"I watched you out the window when you set out," Loretta said. "You were doing an excellent job of correcting her. I think the credit goes to you."

Sean's cheeks grew pink. "You think so?"

"I certainly do. David isn't the only one in this town who's good with dogs. Maybe you'll end up being a trainer, too."

"Dr. Allen is great with dogs, too."

"Of course. He's a veterinarian. They're good with all animals."

"I'm sort of thinking… maybe… I'd like to be a vet. For my career."

Loretta stopped wiping the counters and faced him. "You'd be a wonderful vet, Sean. You've always been calm around medical things—like when your sister had her kidney replacement. If that's what you want, go for it."

"I'll need to get great grades in college."

"You're a straight-A student, now. You're more than capable of that."

"So… I'm smart?"

Loretta walked to him and took his face in her hands. "You're brilliant."

"What'll Frank say? I think he wants one of us to take over Haynes Enterprises."

"Frank will be so proud. Neither of us wants any of you kids to do something just to please us. We want you to follow your dreams."

"Marissa said that—before she left for dance."

"I'm glad. She and I had a long talk earlier, too. Remember—you can come to Frank or me anytime."

Sean nodded. "Where's everybody now?"

"Marissa won't be home for another hour and a half. Grace and Nicole are in her room and the babies are in their swings in the family room."

"Can I go see them?"

"You sure can."

"I won't touch them or anything. I don't want them to cry."

"They're big, healthy babies, Sean. The pediatrician said

they're doing exceptionally well. You don't need to be afraid. You won't hurt them."

His shoulders relaxed, and he stepped into the living room with Daisy at his heels.

Bonnie and Branson were strapped into their individual swings. Their eyes were shut as the swing propelled them forward and back in unison.

Sean approached them, bending over to study their faces. He hadn't been this close to them since their first day home from the hospital.

They bore a striking resemblance to each other—people always commented on it when they saw the twins—but he could tell them apart. Branson's mouth curved up at the corners while Bonnie's eyebrows were set at an infinitesimal diagonal.

Daisy stood next to him as Sean examined their faces. She sniffed at Branson's toes every time the swing brought them to her.

"It's okay, girl," Sean whispered. "Mom says we can't hurt them."

Daisy took a step forward as the swing moved back, following its motion, then quickly retreated as the swing came in her direction.

Branson opened his eyes and locked them on Sean.

"Hey, buddy," Sean said. "It's me—your big bro. I'm gonna show you how to catch a ball and climb that big tree outside the kitchen door."

Daisy touched her nose to Branson's foot.

"And I'll teach you all about dogs. We've got three of

them," he lowered his voice and bent lower, "but the best is Daisy." He gestured with his head. "This one is Daisy."

Daisy leaned forward and licked Branson's hand as the swing brought it within reach.

Branson's hand jerked at the touch of Daisy's tongue.

Sean lunged for Daisy's collar.

Branson's face exploded in a smile.

Daisy licked his hand again.

Branson smiled even wider.

Sean looked from his dog to his brother. He'd heard his mom tell Frank that baby smiles at this age were a response to gas pains. Babies didn't have real, happy smiles until they were older.

He watched Daisy and Branson repeat the cycle.

Sean grinned at the interaction playing out in front of him. His mother was wrong. Branson was smiling at Daisy. He was sure of it.

CHAPTER 22

"*I* finished it this morning while I was waiting at the dentist's office." Maggie spoke into her phone as she walked to her car. "I'd be happy to drop it off at Loretta's. I drive by on my way home."

She pressed her key fob to unlock her door and kept listening. "You did the right thing—inviting her to join the book club. If Frank's working all the time, she needs a change of pace. I'm getting into my car now. I'll talk to you later."

Maggie punched off the call, started her car, and pulled out of the Highpointe College Administration Building parking lot. She pulled onto the street that would take her past the Haynes home on her way to Rosemont.

A quarter mile further on, the street was blocked by a water main break. Signs directed her to a detour. She followed the designated route and skirted an office park.

Maggie knew Haynes Enterprises was located in that office park. If what Susan had told her was true, Frank would still be there. She pulled off the street and wound her way through the buildings until she found Frank's office. The lights were on.

She parked and climbed the steps to the glass door bearing the name Haynes Enterprises in large block letters. She tried the door, only to find it locked.

Maggie used her keys to tap on the glass. She was reaching for her phone to see if she had his number in her contacts when she saw him emerge from his office and cross the dim reception area to the door.

He looked genuinely surprised to see her standing there. "Maggie," he said, turning the deadbolt and opening the door. "What in the world?" He folded the newspaper he'd been holding and put it under his arm.

"May I come in?"

"Is everything okay? Has something happened to Loretta or one of the kids?" His voice was full of alarm as he stepped back to let her in.

"They're fine. I didn't mean to scare you. I came by to drop this off." She held up the paperback copy of a novel. "For Loretta."

Frank stared at her.

"Loretta's joining our book club and this is what we're discussing at our meeting next week. I finished it, so I'm loaning her my copy."

Frank drew his brows together as if he still didn't understand.

"I was going to swing by your house on my way home, but there's a broken water main and a detour. The detour took me close to your office, so I figured you could take it to Loretta." She held the book out to him and he took it from her.

"This also gives me a chance to check on you, Frank. I want to see how you're doing."

Frank shifted his weight from foot to foot, swaying slightly. "I'm fine."

Maggie swept her eyes over his face. "You don't look fine, Frank. You look exhausted."

"Why does everyone keep picking on me? I'm not the one who's spending every waking moment tending to newborns. I'm working long hours here at my business. It's what I've always done. I'm fine."

"I'm not trying to pick on you, Frank." Maggie reached out her hand and he stepped back. "I'm worried about you."

"You don't need to be. Save it for my kids—they have to grow up with a father..." He halted.

" 'A father' what?"

"Nothing. It doesn't matter."

Maggie squared her shoulders. "It does matter. You were about to say something derogatory about yourself."

Frank turned his face away.

"You haven't come to terms with your felony convictions, have you? You're still berating yourself."

Frank didn't respond.

"You need to let that go."

"What would you know about it? You're little miss

perfect, who zoomed into town as a crusading forensic accountant to save Westbury and the town workers' pension fund from the fraud and embezzlement schemes that I was part of."

"You never intended to be part of them. You got caught up in it and were soon in over your head."

"What difference does that make? I was still involved. My kids have a felon for a father."

"You've taken your punishment and fulfilled all the terms the court imposed on you. You've made the required restitution—and then some. Everyone in town knows that. It isn't only about the mistakes you make in life—it's how you make amends, too."

"I can live with that, but I hate that my kids will have to. You don't know what it's like to live under a cloud of disgrace."

"Is that so? What do you think my life was like in California after Paul died of a heart attack and they discovered he'd embezzled millions from Windsor College? He was the president of the college. We were prominent and respected members of the community. All that went away in a flash. Everyone assumed I knew and had been in on it. At the very least, they figured I'd benefited from the money. None of that was true. Suddenly, people who had invited me to dinner at their home a month before wouldn't even say hello to me on the street. It was humiliating."

Frank stopped swaying and faced her. "I guess you do know what I'm feeling. How do I make my thoughts stop? They're on a continual loop in my brain."

"I spent months playing that same loop in my head. I kept telling myself I should have known what Paul was up to. The honest answer is that I didn't. A therapist helped me realize I can't control what other people think of me—that I needed to forgive myself and move on."

Frank's shoulders sagged.

"Maybe you should see a counselor. It's a lot to sort out on your own."

"I don't need to have my head shrunk."

"That's antiquated thinking, Frank," Maggie shot back. "Staying here—hiding away in your office—isn't helping you. Or your family."

"I'm working," he said stiffly.

"You were sitting in your office, reading the paper, weren't you?" She pointed to the newspaper clamped to his side.

He glared at her.

"This isn't fair to you or to your family. Your kids want you. Loretta needs your help and support, too." Her tone softened. "Isolating from the people who love you isn't the way out of this, Frank. Give them a chance to help."

They stood in silence.

"I'll take the book to Loretta," Frank said. "Thanks for bringing it by."

"Think about what I've said. You're miserable and you don't have to be." Maggie walked to her car with a heavy heart.

CHAPTER 23

*L*oretta pulled the lasagna out of the oven and set it on the stovetop. She took a salad from the refrigerator, together with three different bottled dressings. A loaf of Italian bread sat on the counter.

She stepped back and sighed in satisfaction. Her family would have a good meal while she went to book club.

Loretta had been excited about the prospect of an evening out with friends since Susan had first mentioned it. She hadn't had time to read more than the first chapter of Maggie's copy of the book—and she didn't remember much about the characters or the plot. She hoped Susan was right and insightful literary conversation would not be necessary.

The book was in her purse. She'd showered, put on her full makeup, and styled her hair in the afternoon while Ingrid was there. All she needed was for Grace to arrive, and she and Marissa would be on their way. Loretta would drop her daughter off at dance class on her way to Susan's.

Loretta checked the time on her phone. It was unusual for Grace to be late. She noticed the number in the tiny red circle above the messages app. Her heart leapt into her throat as she clicked over to the message and listened. Her fears were realized. Grace had a sore throat and was not coming tonight—and might not be able to work all week.

Loretta raked her hand through her hair and moaned.

"I'm gonna eat before we leave," Marissa said as she came around the corner into the kitchen. She stopped at the sight of her mother.

"What's wrong, Mom?"

"Grace is sick and can't come." Loretta swallowed hard to conceal her disappointment. "I won't be going to book club. You can eat while I put the babies in their car seats. I'll drive you to dance."

"Mom—no. You've been looking forward to this so much. I can stay home with my brothers and sisters."

"You are NOT going to miss out on any more of your activities. Childcare for this family is not your responsibility." Her tone indicated the topic was not up for discussion.

Marissa moved past her mother and served herself a helping of lasagna. "What about..."

"Frank?" Loretta finished her sentence. "I was thinking that, myself."

"He knows you're going to book club. He told me he's happy about it. He'll come home so you can go."

"I'll call him right now," Loretta said. "We'll leave as soon as he gets here. That'll mean you'll be a few minutes late to class. I'm sorry about that."

"No worries, Mom. That won't matter. We warm up in the beginning. I'll do that here, when I'm done eating."

Loretta ran her hand over her eldest daughter's back, and stepped away to call Frank. He answered on the first ring.

"Are you excited about tonight?" he asked.

"I am. Putting on my makeup and fixing my hair makes me feel like a grownup again."

"That's awesome. You deserve a night out."

"I'm glad to hear you say that," Loretta said, "because I need your help."

"Oh?"

"Grace called in sick, so I need you to come home to take care of the kids. I've already fixed dinner, so you won't have to wrangle food for anyone other than the babies. I pumped today and there are bottles for them in the fridge."

Frank didn't reply.

"Frank? Are you there?"

"I'm here. I'm sorry to hear this, sweetheart. And I know how much you've been looking forward to this, but I'm in the middle of second quarter financial statements and—"

Loretta cut him off. "You're always in the middle of something at Haynes Enterprises, Frank. Whatever it is, I'm sure it can wait until the morning."

"These are due to franchise headquarters by the end of the week. They're important."

"I'M IMPORTANT, Frank! My mental and emotional health are important. I want—no, I deserve—to go tonight."

"What about Marissa? Surely she can take care of them for a few hours."

"We've talked about her. It's not her job to babysit her younger siblings. Her troupe is rehearsing for their recital. She needs to be there." Loretta's tone was steely. "These are your children, too, Frank. You need to take hands-on responsibility for them. Supporting them financially isn't all that's required of you."

She paused and waited.

"All right. I'm on my way."

"I need you to leave now. Marissa and I will both be late, as it is. No dilly dallying around, attending to one last thing. Shut down your computer and get out of there."

Frank stabbed at his keyboard. "Did you hear that? I just logged out." He swallowed hard. "I'm sorry, sweetheart. You're right. I'll be there soon."

"Thank you, Frank. Drive safely." Loretta punched off the call.

Frank rushed out the door of Haynes Enterprises, locking it behind him. He checked the lock only once before forcing himself to turn and sprint to his car in the parking lot.

CHAPTER 24

*L*oretta walked along the sidewalk toward Susan's home. The driveway had been full of cars and she'd had to park along the curb, halfway down the street. Every window along the front of the house was open on this balmy, early summer evening.

A chandelier glowed in the room to the left of the front door. Loretta could see a group of women milling around a dining table. Some of them sipped wine while others were filling plates.

Loretta halted at the front door. She hadn't brought anything—other than Maggie's copy of that month's book. Was this a potluck? Should she have brought a dish to share?

She tucked her hair behind her ears and thought back to her conversation with Susan. She hadn't mentioned food— Loretta was sure of it.

Loretta still hung back. She was eager to fit in with this

fun group of women—she didn't want to appear clueless or, worse, rude. Why hadn't she thought to ask what she could bring? She was turning to retreat to her car when Susan flung open the front door.

"Loretta. Hi!" Susan stepped onto the porch. "I thought I saw you walking up the driveway. Where are you going?"

Loretta felt her color rise. "I… I forgot to bring something for the potluck."

"There's nothing for you to bring. Just yourself," Susan said, motioning for Loretta to come inside. "You're just in time. We're getting food. We'll take it onto my back patio to eat and talk—with discussion of the book entirely optional." She chuckled.

Loretta reached into her purse and brought out her wallet. "Do we all chip in for dinner?"

"No. It's potluck."

Loretta moaned. "I knew I should have brought something. I'm so sorry."

"You weren't supposed to. Book Club rule—if you have a newborn at home, or a family member in the hospital, or some other reason that makes rustling up a dish a problem— you're excused from bringing anything."

"You're just saying that to make me feel better."

"No, I'm not. I didn't bring food for the first six months after Julia was born. She had colic, and I was lucky to have groceries in the house, let alone cook something that wasn't simply warmed up in the microwave." Susan put her arm around Loretta's shoulders and drew her inside. "We always have more than enough food. Don't worry about it. We all have times in our lives when we have to let others carry the load for us."

Loretta sniffled and blinked rapidly. "You're sure the others won't be annoyed?"

"Positive."

"There you are," Tonya said, stepping into the foyer. "I thought I heard your voice, Loretta. Come on in and fix a plate. We're all out on the patio, waiting for you. We want to pass your phone around so we can see pictures of those gorgeous twins of yours while you eat."

Loretta's shoulders relaxed.

Susan patted her back. "Food's in here." She pointed to the dining room. "I'll get your drink. We've got white and red wine, iced tea, and water."

"Iced tea, please."

"I'll meet you out back."

Loretta filled her plate with offerings from some of the most talented cooks in Westbury, then stepped through the French doors onto the patio.

The sun was setting, and colorful lanterns strung from one end of the patio to the other glowed in the fading light. The buzz of convivial conversation stopped as the group turned to her.

Joan was the first one on her feet. "Loretta," she cried, setting her plate on a low, glass-topped coffee table and crossing to hug her. "We're so glad you're joining us. We have the best time. And we've all become terrific friends. You're going to love it!"

For the second time that evening, Loretta had to choke back tears.

"We saved you a spot on the sofa, with us," Anita said, patting the empty spot between herself and Judy.

Loretta folded herself into her seat. She put her purse at her feet.

"There's one more rule," Susan said. "We all put our phones on silent."

"But… what if there's an emergency?"

"Who's home with the kids?" Tonya asked.

"Frank."

"Then their dad will take care of it."

Loretta reluctantly reached into her purse and removed her phone. Her fingers hovered on the switch to turn it to silent mode. "What if something happens to Frank?"

"Your family knows where you are. Someone would come here to tell you."

Loretta looked uncertain.

"Honey," Tonya said. "I'm the mother of four—five, if you count that husband of mine."

Laughter coursed around the room.

"George is a wonderful father and very capable, but all of them seem to think there are things only I know—situations only I can handle. That's usually fine, but it gets old, too. For one evening a month—here, at book club—I get to be off the grid. And I like it. It's good for my family, too. I go home refreshed and ready to step back into super-mom mode. Win-win, if you ask me."

Loretta pushed the switch to silent.

"Now," Lyla said, "open your photos and let us ooh and ahh over those babies."

Loretta grinned and complied with the request.

The women ate and drank as the sky cloaked itself in colors of gold, crimson, and purple before settling on black. They discussed the book, with Lyla Kershaw, Sunday Sloan, and Maggie having the most to say. Conversation flowed into discussions of children and husbands, parents and siblings, neighbors and co-workers.

Loretta was laughing with Anita over the antics of Anita's goldendoodle puppy when Sunday crossed the room to her, holding out Loretta's phone.

"I was the last one to see the baby photos. I almost put your phone in my purse, by mistake. We have the same phone case," she said, handing the phone to Loretta. "Your babies are absolutely adorable. Those photos of them holding hands are the cutest things I've ever seen."

"Thank you," Loretta said. "It gets me right here," she touched her fist to her heart, "every time I see them do it." She took the phone from Sunday.

Loretta glanced at the screen as she picked up her purse. The phone icon showed she had eight missed calls. Loretta's jaw tightened. She tapped at the screen. All the calls had been from Frank. "I've got to go," she said, scooting past Anita.

Loretta found Susan and Tonya in the kitchen.

"I had a wonderful time, Susan," Loretta said. "Thank you for inviting me. I'm so glad I came."

"Are you leaving? We were just going to serve dessert."

"It's my grandmother's coconut cream pie," Tonya said.

"A slice of heaven," Susan said. "You won't want to miss it."

Loretta shook her head. "I can't."

"Let me guess," Tonya said. "You looked at your phone and found a dozen missed calls from your family."

Loretta nodded.

"That's what I'm talking about," Tonya said. "Now you see the wisdom of turning your electronic leash off for one evening."

Loretta shrugged.

"You go home and check on them. You'll be too nervous to stay here and enjoy yourself now that you know about the calls." She walked to Loretta and put her hands on her shoulders. "We've all been where you are. And we've done what you're doing."

Loretta gave her a rueful smile.

"Promise me one thing," Tonya said.

"Sure."

"Join us again next month. Book club's at my house. I'll email you my address and the date." Tonya gave her a hug. "Drive safely. You're going to find that everything's fine."

"Thank you," Loretta said. "Both of you." She headed for the foyer, then spun around, Maggie's copy of the book in her hand.

"You can leave it on the counter over there." Susan pointed. "I'll make sure Mom gets it. Now go—and don't worry about a thing."

CHAPTER 25

Frank hung up before leaving another voice mail message. Either Loretta didn't have her phone on her or she was ignoring his calls. He held Bonnie against his shoulder, rubbing her back and bouncing her as she wailed inconsolably. He'd done something wrong. He knew it.

He'd given Branson his bottle without incident, but Bonnie had been another story. She'd turned her head from side to side every time he'd offered her the nipple. When he'd burped her after she'd finally taken an ounce or two, she'd thrown it all up. The collar of his shirt was still damp and sticky. The aroma of vomited milk clung to him.

"What's wrong with her, Daddy?" Nicole stood in the doorway of the nursery. "She never cries like that."

"I don't know." Frank was curt.

"It's time for my story. Are you going to read to me?"

"I can't right now, can I?" He paced as he continued to bounce Bonnie. "You'll have to go to bed without a story tonight."

Nicole's shoulders drooped.

"I'm sorry, sweetie. It's just for tonight."

Nicole nodded and shuffled off.

Frank looked at his watch. It was 8:30. Loretta told him she'd be home by ten. Marissa had texted that she was getting a ride home from dance and would be back by nine. Maybe she'd know what was wrong with Bonnie. He only had to hold on for another half hour.

The doorbell rang. Sally, Snowball, and Daisy all ran to the door, barking their heads off.

Frank cursed under his breath. Who in the world was at his door at this time of night? If the dogs woke Branson, he didn't know what he was going to do.

Frank met up with Sean as he came out of his bedroom. "Go shut up the dogs," Frank ordered as they raced down the hall toward the commotion at the door.

They rounded the corner into the foyer.

"Quiet!" Sean commanded. The dogs stopped barking. "I'll put them outside," Sean said. "Come on, guys."

The dogs followed him into the kitchen.

Frank yanked open the door.

Bonnie filled her lungs and cried even harder.

Gloria and Glenn stood on his doorstep. Glenn held an oversize crock-pot and Gloria carried a plate of cookies. The octogenarian couple smiled at him.

"What...?" Frank sputtered.

"Didn't Loretta tell you?" Gloria asked.

Frank drew his brows together. "Tell me what?"

"That we'd be dropping by tonight after choir practice to drop off this crock-pot. I never use it anymore and put it up for sale on one of those community apps." Gloria glowed with pride at mastering such a modern way of doing things. "Loretta bought it. With your big family, she'll use it a lot."

Glenn nodded at the appliance in his hands. "The instructions are inside it. Gloria keeps everything." He cast an admiring glance at his wife.

"And I baked cookies this afternoon, so I brought you some."

"That's so nice of you," Frank said, raising his voice to be heard above Bonnie's wailing. "Do you mind bringing them into the kitchen? I've got my hands full."

He led the way into the kitchen.

Gloria put the cookies on the counter.

Frank turned to her, his eyes full of misery. "You had children, didn't you?"

"Nine, in fact. And twenty-one grandchildren," Gloria replied.

"What's wrong with her? She's been crying like this for at least forty-five minutes."

"Loretta's out, isn't she? She told me she was going to book club when we made arrangements about the crock-pot this afternoon."

Frank nodded. "She won't be home for another hour. What'll I do if I can't get her to stop crying? I've called but Loretta doesn't answer. I don't know... I just don't know."

His words came faster and faster. "Maybe I should take her to the emergency room?"

"Goodness," Gloria said. "I don't think you need to do that. May I?" She held out her arms and Frank placed Bonnie into them. "Tell me what you've done so far."

Frank relayed the less-than-successful feeding with the bottle.

Bonnie kept crying.

"Sounds to me like she might have gotten an air bubble in her tummy with that bottle. That's why she threw up." Gloria looked into the red, damp face of the furious infant. She held Bonnie's forehead to her cheek. "She doesn't have a fever. I think she's just hungry. Do you have another bottle?"

"There's milk in the freezer. I have no idea what to do with it. Loretta had the bottles ready for me in the refrigerator when I got home."

He opened the freezer and removed a small plastic bag of breast milk. "Do you know how to make a bottle?"

Gloria chuckled. "I do. I'm going to tell you how, so you can make them from now on."

"I'm not so sure…"

Glenn clapped him on the back. "You can do this, Frank. I've made and given bottles to my kids and grandkids. If I can do it, you can do it."

"Where are the bottles and nipples?" Gloria asked.

"Uh… I'm not sure." Frank began opening cupboards and drawers. A stack of glassware in one of the cupboards was leaning at a precarious angle. Frank stopped his search to restack and straighten them.

Gloria perched on a stool at the kitchen island and cleared her throat. "I think they're in that cupboard you just opened," she said.

Frank pulled out the necessary supplies and Gloria instructed him in the simple steps to thaw the milk and assemble the bottle.

"That was easier than I thought it would be," Frank said, handing Gloria the bottle.

Gloria squeezed a drop of milk onto the nipple and rubbed it on Bonnie's lip.

Bonnie stopped crying.

Gloria inclined Bonnie so her head was higher than her feet.

Bonnie latched onto the bottle and sucked greedily.

Frank hovered over her shoulder

"Here's the thing," Gloria said, glancing up at Frank. "Make sure that there's milk filling the nipple at all times. If you hold the bottle at the wrong angle, air will get in and she'll suck it into her tummy. That's what happened. She was crying because she was hungry."

Frank put his elbows on the kitchen island and rested his head in his hands. "Thank God. I thought I'd done something to her—or that she'd gotten horribly sick suddenly. You hear about that on the news all the time."

"Your babies are thriving, Frank. I understand it's natural to be worried about them, but don't imagine the worst at every turn. It'll take all the joy out of parenting."

Bonnie finished the bottle.

Gloria burped her and held out the now contented infant to Frank.

He held Bonnie against his chest, and she burrowed under his chin. "Thank you so much. I'm glad you came by. I don't know what I would have done without your help."

"You'd have survived just fine," Gloria said. "Crying until Loretta came home wouldn't have hurt her. If I can offer another unsolicited piece of advice?" She gave him an encouraging smile. "Relax and enjoy this experience. You'll make mistakes. Forgive yourself. The most important thing a parent can do is love their children, listen to their children, and encourage their children."

"We'd better be on our way," Glenn said. "Choir practice is our one late night during the week. We're usually in bed by now."

Frank—and a sleeping Bonnie—walked them to the door.

"IT's a good thing we stopped by when we did," Glenn said to Gloria as they pulled out of the driveway. "Frank looked like he was freaking out."

"He was." Gloria inhaled slowly.

Glenn glanced at her. "He's never given a bottle to a baby before. That would throw anyone for a loop."

"I guess." Gloria's tone was contemplative.

"The baby was fine. She went to sleep the minute she finished that bottle."

"That's true."

"Then why do you sound worried about something?"

"You know me so well, don't you?"

"I can tell by the way you're breathing that you've got something on your mind." He reached across the console to take her hand. "So, tell me."

"I'm uneasy, Glenn. Something's wrong."

"You said yourself that Bonnie wasn't sick. What're you talking about?"

"I'm not worried about those babies. It's Frank that concerns me."

"He was frazzled by a crying baby. That's all."

"It's more than that." She shifted in her seat to look at Glenn. "You've known Frank longer—and better—than I have. Did you notice anything different about him?"

"He had sour milk spit-up on his shirt?"

"I'm serious, Glenn. This could be important. I want you to think about Frank. Did anything strike you as out of the ordinary?"

"He's lost weight since the last time I saw him."

"How much?"

Glenn inhaled slowly. "I don't know—maybe twenty pounds. It's noticeable, that's for sure."

"When was the last time you saw him?"

"The night of Loretta's baby shower—when the guys got together with Frank to help him finish the nursery."

"That was six weeks ago. Twenty pounds is a lot to lose in six weeks."

Glenn nodded in agreement.

"Did you see him stop to tidy the glassware while he was looking for the nipples and bottles?"

"Yeah. I remember thinking, 'What are you doing? Leave that for later.'"

"Exactly. He was mesmerized by restoring order to that shelf. If I hadn't interrupted him by telling him I'd seen what we needed in the cupboard he'd just opened, I think he might have kept on stacking and restacking the glassware."

"Okay... How is wanting a neat cupboard a problem?"

"It's not, but I think it's odd. Frank's working all the time and he's developed obsessive-compulsive habits. I wonder if he's depressed."

Glenn glanced at her again. "I don't know, sweetheart. You may be blowing things out of proportion. Besides—he was home tonight. He isn't working himself to death."

"That's not what Loretta told me when I called this afternoon. I asked her how it's been going and she said that he's working late every night. If she hadn't hired Grace to be a mother's helper, she'd have lost her mind."

"Hmmm..." Glenn shrugged. "I'm not sure what we can do about it."

"I've been thinking. Why don't you call him and invite him to lunch? Maybe with you and Tim Knudsen. Frank and Tim are friends, aren't they?"

"They are. What are we supposed to do at lunch? Ask him how he's feeling? That'd be hard for me to do. Guys don't yack about personal stuff like you women do."

"And you're the worse for it, I can tell you that." She pursed her lips. "How about this: take him to lunch and see if he eats anything? If he just picks at his food, ask him about that. And his weight loss. Surely you can do that?"

Glenn nodded. "Would that make you feel better?"

"It would. I've seen how people suffer from depression. If Frank has it, I want to suggest he gets help."

"That's a kind thing to do for him, honey."

"It's not just for him. Loretta and his kids are affected, too."

"You've convinced me. I'll call Frank in the morning."

"And if you can get him talking about anything else, do it."

"Tim and I can find out if he's working long hours. I don't know how I'd ask him if he's OCD."

"You probably won't have to. If he is, you'll notice him doing something repetitive."

"I feel like I'll be spying on him. That doesn't seem right."

"You'll be caring for a friend who needs your help. That's always the right thing to do."

LORETTA RAN down the hallway to find Frank sitting on the family room sofa, a baby nestled under each arm. His head was tilted back, his mouth was open, and he was asleep. "Frank," Loretta cried breathlessly. "I got here as fast as I could."

He opened his eyes slowly. "Hi, sweetheart. Did you have fun?"

"I did—until I saw I had eight missed calls from you. I left right away and tried calling you all the way home. You never picked up."

"Sorry," he said sleepily.

"You scared me to death, Frank! What in the world were you calling about?"

He swallowed hard, debating whether to tell her about his panic over Bonnie, and Gloria's stepping in to rescue him. He decided that story didn't need to be shared.

"It doesn't matter—it all got handled." He slid over as she sat down next to him.

"I've got to nurse these guys right now. I haven't gone this long without feeding them and I'm about to burst."

He quickly handed the babies to Loretta. She had them situated in the blink of an eye.

"So—tell me about your night," Loretta said. "Did Marissa get home okay?"

"Right on time. She was beat and headed straight to bed. They're all asleep." He leaned toward Loretta and planted a kiss on her cheek. "Gloria and Glenn dropped off a crock-pot and some cookies she baked."

"I'm sorry I forgot to tell you they'd be stopping by. That was nice of her to bring cookies. She's amazing, isn't she?"

Frank nodded. He knew better than anyone how amazing Gloria was.

CHAPTER 26

"Ready to go?" Josh asked Sunday when she answered her door on Saturday night. He leaned in and kissed her. "The movie starts in half an hour. I thought we'd grab something to eat after."

"I know that's our plan," Sunday said, "but we need to change it." She took his hand as they walked to his car. "I hope you don't mind, but I've agreed to do something else. If you don't want to, I'll do it myself."

"Of course I want to be with you. Why wouldn't I? What're we doing?"

Sunday took a deep breath before continuing. "Babysitting."

Josh took a step back. "Seriously?"

Sunday nodded. "We're taking care of Bonnie and Branson so the rest of the family can go to Marissa's dance recital."

"Frank and Loretta's twins?"

"Yep."

"Okay. I didn't know you were close to them."

"I'm not, really. Loretta just joined our book club and I'm getting to know her there."

Josh opened the car door for her. "This is making less sense to me as you keep explaining."

Sunday laughed. "Here's what happened. Grace is their babysitter, but she's sick with a terrible cold. Susan was going to fill in, but Julia had the sniffles last week and now Susan and Maggie are in bed with it. Your mom was going to cover for them. She just called me because she has a scratchy throat and is running a fever."

"Are we the only healthy adults in Westbury? Other than Frank, Loretta, and their older kids?"

Sunday laughed. "Apparently. I know I should have called to ask you before I agreed to step in, but there wasn't time. I really like Loretta and haven't done much to help her. Like I said—if you don't want any part of this, I can handle it by myself."

"And—like I told you—I want to be with you. I don't care what we do. But," he turned to her, his tone serious, "I don't know the first thing about babies. I'm happy to be there with you, but don't expect me to be very useful."

Sunday leaned across the console and kissed his cheek. "That makes two of us. How hard can it be? We'll figure it out, together." She gave him the address, and they set out.

Twenty minutes later, after a flurry of barking dogs, detailed lists of written instructions concerning the babies, and a mad dash to find Sean's shoes, the family had departed. Sunday and Josh faced each other. She cradled Bonnie while he held Branson.

"Gosh," Sunday said. "That was intense."

"Sort of like the circus leaving town," Josh quipped.

The dogs circled at their feet.

"What're we supposed to do now?" Josh asked.

Bonnie tooted, and the air became saturated with an unwelcome odor.

"I guess we've got our answer," Sunday said.

"I'm glad it's your baby and not mine," Josh teased, trailing after Sunday as they headed to the nursery.

Branson followed his sister's lead.

"Looks like you spoke too soon." Sunday looked over her shoulder at Josh and grinned.

They approached the changing table together.

"This can't be difficult. Right?" Josh said.

"There are diapers on the shelf below and wipes right there," Sunday said, pointing.

"Ladies first," Josh said.

Sunday pursed her lips. "Maybe we should do some research. Like watch a YouTube video—or a couple of videos."

"That's my librarian girlfriend for you," Josh chided.

"It can't hurt," Sunday defended herself.

"Of course not." He shifted Branson to his left hip and manipulated his phone with his right hand.

Sunday leaned into him, and they were soon watching videos on the best diaper changing techniques.

"That doesn't look too hard," Sunday said. "We can do this."

"I'm glad they said to cover a boy baby with a diaper. I'd never have thought of that on my own," Josh said.

"No. I'd have learned that the hard way." She took a deep breath and laid Bonnie on the changing table. In a matter of minutes, she'd handled the task. She stepped back. "Do you want to switch babies? This whole thing was my idea, so I'll change him."

"And not practice the baby diapering skills I've just learned? Not on your life. As a matter of fact, I plan to beat your time."

"Are you serious? You timed me?"

Josh nodded, holding his phone out to her to read the screen. "The time to beat is eight minutes, thirteen seconds." He laid Branson on the changing table and started the stopwatch function.

Josh worked with focused precision. He fastened the tabs on the clean diaper and put the dirty one in the diaper pail, then looked at his phone. "Six minutes, fifty-nine seconds. The winning team is Josh and Branson!"

Sunday laughed. "Now that I know we're competing, I'll speed up next time. If there is a next time—maybe we won't have to change them again before the family gets home."

"What do we do now?"

"We're supposed to put them to bed."

"Branson is already asleep," Josh said. "He's really sweet. I can see the appeal of these guys."

"Bonnie's zonked out, too," Sunday said. "I think we should hold them for a while."

"Let's take them onto the porch," Josh said. "It's a beautiful night."

"I saw one of those old-fashioned gliders out there. I love those things. We can sit there and swing the babies."

"I like the sound of that."

"Just for a little while. We'll put them in their beds soon."

Sunday and Josh carried their sweet-smelling cargos to the glider and carefully settled into it.

Josh set the swing to rocking.

They sat together in companionable silence and watched the evening slip into night. The moon peeked over the treetops. Fireflies broke the darkness with bursts of yellow-green.

"This is so peaceful," Josh said.

"I was thinking the same thing."

"I had a crazy busy week. Sitting here, with you and these babies, is incredibly relaxing."

"I couldn't agree more," she said. "I'm glad this didn't turn out to be a dud of a date."

Josh took her hand in his. "Anytime I'm with you is perfect."

"I love you," she replied. "You're always so positive."

"You know what would make this more perfect?" He stared into the yard.

Sunday glanced at him. "If you could catch some of those lightning bugs?"

Josh grinned ear to ear. "You read my mind."

"We'll put it on the list for our next date."

"Seriously?"

"Yep. If babysitting has been on the list, we can add that."

"I love you back, Sunday Sloan."

CHAPTER 27

"*H*e was going to meet us here," Tim Knudsen said to the woman behind the welcome desk at Forever Friends.

"Frank said he'd help us pick out a dog that would be a good fit for our ten-year-old grandson," Nancy Knudsen chimed in.

"I'm sorry, but Mr. Haynes hasn't been in since he and his wife had the twins."

"I'll call him," Tim said, steering Nancy away from the desk. He greeted Frank warmly when he answered. Tim's smile evaporated as he listened. "I understand you need to complete your financial statements so you can send them in, but… you knew about that deadline three days ago when we set this up."

Nancy glanced at her husband and raised her brows. She

could hear Frank's vociferous response but couldn't make out the words.

"Of course I know what you're doing is important. But our grandson's birthday is today, and we told him we'd have a dog for him. He's counting on us. Neither of us has had dogs—Nancy's allergic. We don't know what to look for. He needs one that's calm and friendly—that'll be easy to train. We promised his parents we wouldn't bring home an animal with aggression issues. I'm sorry if I sound upset, Frank, but you're leaving us in the lurch."

Tim continued to listen and nodded. "Okay. I'll ask for David Wheeler. I know he's the boy that takes his therapy dog to nursing homes and the hospital."

Tim punched off the call. He took Nancy's arm and led them back to the welcome desk. "Is David Wheeler here?"

The woman smiled. "David is always here. Would you like me to call him?"

"Please. Tell him Tim and Nancy Knudsen are here to adopt a dog and that Frank said he could help us find the right one."

David soon appeared in the reception area. "You must be Frank's friends?" David asked as Tim and Nancy smiled at him.

"We are." Tim extended his hand, introduced himself and his wife, and told David what they were looking for.

"Tell me more about your grandson," David said.

"He's a studious, sweet boy," Nancy said. "Shy and sensitive." Her eyes suddenly filled with tears. She pulled out a tissue and blotted her eyes.

David put his hand on her elbow and looked at Tim.

"His father—our son-in-law—is deployed overseas, and Zack isn't handling it well. He misses his dad, and he's become withdrawn and surly," Tim said. "Our daughter took him to a counselor, and she suggested a dog could help our grandson cope. She said that dogs really are man's best friends."

"The counselor is right. I know that from personal experience. I got Dodger after my dad died. That dog turned my life around."

He led them through a door to a long bank of kennels.

"All the dogs up for adoption are in here. You can go up and down the aisle. Information about each dog is on the card attached to the front of the kennel."

"Is this where you got Dodger?" Nancy asked, walking up to the first cage and peering inside at a Pekinese. "I've heard Gloria and Glenn talk about him. He's a celebrity at Fairview Terraces. You both are."

David smiled. "I did. Glenn decided I needed a dog, and we came to Forever Friends to get him."

"A friendly dog, like Dodger, is what we'd like," Nancy said.

"You don't care about breed?"

"Nope," Nancy replied. "If you have a suggestion, we'd be grateful. They all look cute to me. I don't know what to look for."

David narrowed his eyes in thought. "There's a mutt at the end of the row. He was a stray that someone dropped off." He walked toward the dog's kennel. "A true crossbreed. He's forty pounds and we believe he's two."

"How can you tell that?"

"We look at the dog's teeth. The state of their teeth helps us estimate their age." David stopped in front of the kennel.

A medium-size dog with a curly brown and white coat, long floppy ears, and soulful brown eyes stuck his wet black nose through the grate to greet them. He swished his tail against the concrete floor of the kennel.

Tim stuck his fingers through the wire to scratch his muzzle. The dog licked his hand in appreciation.

"He's friendly to everyone, good with other dogs, and smart as a whip," David continued. "I've spent a lot of time with him. I'm surprised he hasn't been adopted yet. He's even housebroken and leash trained. He must have been someone's pet, but he didn't have a collar and he wasn't microchipped. We couldn't find his owner and no one claimed him. If I was getting a dog, he'd be my pick. Hands down."

"That's good enough for me," Nancy said. "He seems very sweet. And calm."

"Do you want to take him to a get-acquainted room? I can let the three of you spend time together."

Tim and Nancy looked at each other and shrugged.

"I don't think we need to. This guy is the one."

"You won't be sorry. Your grandson is going to be the happiest kid in town." David unlocked the kennel and slipped a leash around the dog's neck. "What'd I tell you this morning, buddy? Today was going to be your day. You're going to your forever home!"

The dog sprang to his feet, wagging his tail with gravitational force.

"They know," David said to Nancy and Tim. "You can tell that he understands he's found his family."

Nancy took the soggy tissue from the pocket of her cardigan and dabbed at her eyes again.

"I'll take you to the adoption area to fill out the paperwork."

"Thank you, David," Tim said. "When you see Frank, be sure to let him know what a great place this is."

"I haven't seen or talked to Frank since he had the babies. He doesn't come around here anymore."

"I thought maybe you were in contact with him. He just told me you're running the place for him."

"I'm doing my best. I've got some questions for him, but he doesn't have time."

"If you don't mind my saying, that's a lot of responsibility to put on the shoulders of someone your age," Tim said.

David shrugged. "I've called, but he won't answer. I send emails and he doesn't respond." They reached the adoption area. "Anyway—I'll leave you here. I'm happy you're taking this guy." He dropped to one knee and rubbed the dog behind the ears. "Be good to Zack," he said. "Live your best happy-dog life."

CHAPTER 28

$\mathcal{D}$ avid noted the boy loping toward the glass entry doors to Forever Friends. The friendly mutt that Tim and Nancy had adopted for their grandson trotted at his side. Tim walked behind them.

David pushed the door open. "You must be Zack?"

The boy nodded.

"You're the only ones signed up for today's complimentary dog training session," David said. He looked past Zack to address Tim. "Do you want to come in with us?"

Tim shook his head. "If you don't mind, I have calls to make. One of my clients is putting an offer on a house this morning."

"Sure," David said. "We'll probably work for forty-five minutes."

"I'll be waiting in my car." Tim pointed to his luxury SUV

in the parking lot. "Take your time. And good luck." He brought his phone to his ear and headed toward his car.

"Follow me," David said. "We'll work in the exercise area out back." He squatted next to the dog to rub his ears. "What'd you name this guy?"

"Sparky."

"That's a great name. It suits him." He held the dog's muzzle. "What do you think of that? Do you know your name, Sparky?"

The dog uttered a short woof.

David stood. "He knows his name, doesn't he?"

"Yep. He got it right away."

"That's terrific. I knew he was smart. Some dogs struggle to learn their names."

They walked through Forever Friends and out to the grassy area behind the building.

Sparky strained at the leash as they walked by the kennels.

"He's never done that before," Zack said, pulling him back.

"He remembers being in one of them," David gestured to the kennels. "He doesn't want to go back. We'll walk around the side of the building when we're done."

"You're never going back there, boy." Zack spoke reassuringly. "You're with me, now."

David smiled. "Let's see what he'll do for you. Then we'll decide what he still needs to learn. Can he sit?"

Zack commanded Sparky to sit, and he instantly complied.

"That's awesome," David said. "Any accidents at home?"

"Nope. He scratches at the door when he wants to go out."

"We already know he's leash trained. How about the recall? Does he come when he's called?"

Zack gave the command.

Sparky stood and looked from Zack to David.

"All right. That's what we'll work on. It's critically important for a dog to come when called. Their safety may depend on it."

"Like stopping him from running away?"

"Yes. You can't rely on any of the commands to work in every situation. I never recommend walking him off-leash. If he sees a squirrel across the road and runs after it, you may not be able to stop him with a command." He locked eyes with Zack. "It's your responsibility to maintain control of your dog and to keep him safe."

"I understand." Zack's tone was serious.

"How old are you?"

"I just turned ten. Gramma and Gramps got Sparky for me for my birthday."

"You seem very grown up. I think you'll be a responsible dog owner."

Zack flushed with the compliment. "Thanks."

"To teach Sparky to come, put him in a sit."

Zack did as David directed.

"Now you hold on to the end of the leash and step back from Sparky, as far as the leash will allow."

Zack positioned himself five feet from Sparky.

Sparky began to get to his feet.

"Correct him. Tell him to sit."

"Sparky, sit."

The dog lowered his rear haunches back to the ground.

"Say his name, tug on the leash, and command him to come. All at the same time."

Zack followed the instructions, and Sparky came to him.

"Tell him to sit and that he's a very good boy. Be real excited about it. Rub him up. He needs to feel like he's done the best thing in the world."

"Good boy, Sparky!" Zack threw his arms around the dog's neck and rubbed from his ears to his back.

Sparky swept his tail along the ground.

"I've got training treats in my jeans pocket," Zack said. "Should I give him one?"

"Great idea. How'd you learn about training treats?"

"I read about dog training online."

"I'm impressed," David complimented the boy. "Let's try it a couple more times, with you tugging on the leash when you give the command. Be sure to praise him when he's successful."

Zack and Sparky ran through the exercise four more times, with complete success.

"Now let's try it without tugging on the leash. You'll use this command when he's off leash. Drop the leash and try it again. Call his name and tell him to come."

Sparky came to Zack on the first try and jumped up, resting his paws on Zack's hips. Zack started to praise him.

"No," David interrupted. "Push him off and tell him to get

down. You don't want Sparky jumping on people. He's supposed to come and sit in front of you. Put him into a sit and walk away from him."

Zack followed David's instructions, and they tried again. This time, Sparky sat as soon as he reached his master.

Another four iterations of the exercise were perfectly executed.

"The two of you are killing it! Well done." David stroked Sparky's back. "I think this is enough for one day. Dogs get tired and their attention wanders. There's no point in setting Sparky up for failure."

"What else do we need to learn?"

"Our free lessons include teaching the down stay command. We'll do that next time."

"What about shaking hands and rolling over?"

David laughed. "Those are cool tricks. If we're the only ones here next lesson, I can show you how to train him to do those. You'll have to work on them at home to get them to stick."

"That'd be great. I like working with him."

"Your homework—for the two of you—before our next lesson is to reinforce sit and come. Five repetitions of each every day. Can you do that?"

"Sure. When do we come back?"

"I'm the only trainer and I'm supposed to be out of town next week. But something's come up, so I may be here after all—I don't know yet." David motioned for Zack and Sparky to follow him. "Let's go talk to your grandfather."

They rounded the corner and ran into Tim on his way to the door.

"I finished my calls and was hoping to see you work," Tim said.

"They're doing great," David said. "Zack's a natural."

Zack grinned. "Wanna see him sit and come?"

"Sure," Tim said.

Zack and Sparky executed the commands.

"I may ask the two of you to come back to demonstrate at future lessons," David said. "That's very impressive."

"That'd be cool. We'd do that." Zack pressed his shoulders back.

"So, they're all done?" Tim asked.

"They need one more lesson on the basics," David said. "We usually do lessons once a week. I was planning to take next week off to go to California. I have to look for a place to live when I move there next month."

"Frank told me you were going to spend three years there —going to college and working at the Guide Dog Center. You'll be in the apprenticeship program?"

"Eventually—I'll start by cleaning kennels." David pursed his lips. "Did you talk to Frank recently?"

Tim shook his head. "We haven't spoken in at least a month." He looked at David. "He still isn't stopping by Forever Friends?"

"No. I called him yesterday and again this morning, but he doesn't answer. He knows I planned to be gone next week, but now I'll be out most of this week, too. I have a family emergency."

"I'm sorry to hear that. Can I help?"

"No. My mom missed the bottom rung of the ladder when she was washing windows. She fell and sprained her ankle."

"Ladders are one of the leading causes of household accidents," Tim said. "I'm sorry to hear that. Is she okay?"

"Not really. It's a bad sprain. She broke bones in her foot, too. She can't put any weight on it. As soon as the swelling comes down, they'll decide if they have to operate."

"That sounds serious."

"Our next-door neighbor is staying with her now while I'm here for our lesson. My aunt is flying in the day after tomorrow to stay with us. I need to go home now to take care of Mom." David ran his hand through his hair. "Our office manager is on vacation this week and now I have to be gone, too. There's no one to pick up the slack and I can't reach Frank."

"I may see him later. Glenn and I were planning to take him to lunch." Tim cocked his head to one side. "Would you like me to mention all this to him?"

"That'd be great. At least he's still talking to his friends. I'm glad he's going to lunch."

"We don't have plans, actually. Glenn and I will just show up and insist he come with us."

"Good luck with that," David said.

"We heard he's isolating himself. Anyway—you'll be in California next week, so Zack's next lesson will be the week after that?"

"I doubt I'll go now. Mom was coming with me, but she

can't after this fall. I'm only seventeen—I just graduated from high school. I don't know how to find and rent an apartment here, let alone in another state."

Tim narrowed his eyes and rubbed his chin. "You'll need help, that's for sure."

"If I'm in Westbury next week—and it looks like I will be —and my aunt is helping with Mom, I'll give these guys"—he gestured to Zack and Sparky—"another lesson. Is your number on the adoption records?"

Tim nodded.

"I'll let you know," David said.

"I hope—for your sake—that we'll have to wait another week for that lesson. And I hope your mom is back on her feet soon." Tim led Zack and his dog toward the car.

David was almost out of view when Tim turned back and called to him. "Have you canceled your plane tickets?"

David shook his head. "Not yet."

"Don't," Tim called back.

"Why?" David replied.

"I've got an idea." He held up his phone and waggled it. "Give me some time. I'll call you after lunch."

David watched as his star students marched with newfound confidence to Tim's car.

CHAPTER 29

*J*im pulled into the parking lot at Haynes Enterprises. "You really think Frank might be depressed?" He angled his car into the first available spot.

"I'm not sure," Glenn said. "Gloria is really worried about him. She's convinced. I promised her I'd take Frank to lunch to find out how he's feeling."

"That's a tall order. Frank isn't the kind of guy who wears his heart on his sleeve."

"I warned Gloria about that, but she insisted I try. That's why I called you. It'll be easier to get him talking if there's two of us. I won't feel like I'm cross-examining a witness."

Tim chuckled. "Let's hope it doesn't get to that."

"You're closer to him than I am, anyway."

"We talked every day when he was helping sell assets for the town workers' pension fund—while he was performing the community service part of his sentence. We finished everything shortly after the babies were born. I've barely spoken to him since." Tim shook his head. "I thought he was just too busy with Loretta and the kids. It never occurred to me he might be... well... in trouble."

"I'm glad you saw David at the shelter this morning. Frank's devoted to that boy. If Frank declines our invitation, we can try to use David to change his mind."

"It's a plan." Tim consulted his watch. "It's almost noon. We'd better get in there."

Glenn sighed heavily as he reached for the passenger door handle. "Let's hope Gloria's fears are unfounded."

"And that the only negative take-away from this lunch is that I break my diet and eat a piece of pie after my healthy salad."

Glenn chuckled. "If you do, I won't say a word to Gloria. Nancy isn't going to find out because of me."

"That's a good friend." Tim got out of the car. "Let's find out what's going on with our other good friend, Frank."

Mary greeted the two men as they stepped through the double glass doors bearing the Haynes Enterprises' name.

"We're here to see Frank," Tim said.

"Do you have an appointment?" Mary tapped her keyboard. "I don't see one on his calendar."

"We're friends of his," Glenn said, giving her their names. "We were in the neighborhood and thought we'd drop in and take him to lunch."

Mary smiled at the earnest faces of the men in front of her. "I'm afraid Mr. Haynes is very busy right now. He's asked me to hold his calls."

"It's all right," Glenn insisted. "He'll want to see us."

"I'm not to disturb him."

Tim crossed to the closed door to Frank's office.

"I wouldn't, sir," Mary called to him.

"We worked together on the pension fund properties," Tim said. "Do you remember me?"

Mary nodded, her eyes wide in alarm as Tim raised his hand and knocked on the door.

"What!?" Frank bellowed from behind the door.

Tim knocked again.

The ensuing silence was broken by heavy footsteps inside Frank's office.

Glenn went to stand with Tim.

Frank flung the door open. "I told you..." His tone was curt, and his chest was puffed out. He stopped abruptly when he saw his friends.

"Hey, Frank," Tim said, extending his hand.

Frank shook it before turning to Glenn and doing the same.

"What're you two doing here?"

"We were driving by and decided to pick you up for lunch," Glenn said. "If you don't have plans." He looked past Frank at the neat stacks of papers on his desk. "It looks like you weren't planning to go anywhere."

"No. As you can see, I've got..."

Tim cut him off. "It's Rueben day at Pete's. You and I used to grab a Reuben once a week. Nancy's got me on a strict diet, and I haven't had one since we stopped going. I need to fix that."

A ghost of a smile played on Frank's lips. "Pete's Reubens are the best." He shook his head. "I'm sorry, guys, but I'm buried."

"You've got to eat, Frank. We'll have you back in an hour. Besides, I haven't seen pictures of your babies," Tim said.

Frank inhaled slowly.

"We need to talk about David, too. I just heard about his mother," Tim continued.

Frank's head snapped up. "What's happened to Jackie?"

"Come on," Glenn said, moving to the door. "We'll fill you in on the way."

Frank shuffled after him.

"We'll be back," Tim said to Mary as he held the door for Glenn and Frank. The three men left the building without seeing the smile spread across Mary's face.

PETE SET three Reuben sandwiches on the table. "I'm glad to see you, Frank," he said. "This is the first time you've been in since your twins were born. Congratulations."

"Thank you," Frank said, reaching for his phone. "Would you like to see photos?"

"Sure," Pete said, taking the phone and scrolling. "People teased me that I must have bought extra cloud storage for all the photos I took of our baby. I think you've got me beat." He returned the phone to Frank. "They're adorable. Branson looks just like you and I can see a lot of Loretta in Bonnie."

"I haven't seen them yet," Glenn said, intercepting the phone.

"I'll be back to check on you. Enjoy," Pete said before heading toward the kitchen.

Glenn looked at the photos. "You've got yourself a wonderful family, Frank. You deserve this. Be proud of yourself."

"Thank you." Frank turned his face quickly aside.

"This sandwich is as good as I remember," Tim said. "Much better than the salad I should have ordered. What do you think, Frank? Still the best Reuben you've ever had?"

Frank nibbled at his sandwich before putting it back on his plate. "I don't know. Nothing tastes good to me anymore."

"You've lost a lot of weight since I last saw you," Tim observed.

"I'm not trying to. I'm just not hungry."

"I wish I had that problem," Tim said. He and Glenn exchanged glances.

"How are things going?" Glenn asked.

"Fine. The babies are a lot of extra work, but Loretta's amazing. She's keeping everything going at home. The big kids are thriving at school. Marissa is involved in a competitive dance troupe. Sean is working at Forever Friends with David. And Nicole—well—she's a happy little girl. We have a day nanny and an after-school helper, but Loretta still manages it all. She's incredible."

"Glad to hear it," Glenn said. "Loretta *is* amazing—but I

was asking about you. How do you feel these days? Your world has been turned upside down."

Frank straightened his silverware, aligning each piece so that the tip of each handle was an inch from the table's edge. He folded and unfolded his napkin. "I'm fine. Busy at work."

Tim arched a brow at Glenn.

Glenn nodded his acknowledgment that he'd noted Frank's behavior.

"How's that going? Every time I drive by one of your fast-food franchises, the parking lot is full. I wait in line at the pick-up window every morning for my first cup of coffee," Tim said. "I know you're busy."

"Sales are great. Revenues are soaring."

"Gloria mentioned that you're working late a lot," Glenn began.

Frank cut him off. "So, what if I am? That's why we're doing so well."

Glenn held up a hand. "I'm not criticizing."

"I'm now supporting a family of seven. I need to make sure my business continues to do well." Frank looked at his watch and took a sip of his tea.

"Do you mind if I order a piece of today's special pie?" Tim said. "It's homemade peach. My favorite."

"You say every pie is your favorite," Glenn teased. "I'm in. Shall we make it three pieces, Frank?"

Frank shook his head no. "You go ahead."

Tim flagged down Pete and ordered two pieces of the pie —with ice cream.

"Do either of you know what David's going to do about finding a place to live since Jackie can't travel?" Frank asked.

"I've got three closings next week, so I can't take him," Tim said. "Besides, he's only just met me."

"Gloria is having cataract surgery. I can't be away either," Glenn said.

Frank pursed his lips. "I'll take him to California to look for a place to live."

"You don't want to leave your family right now," Glenn said.

"I'm going to California next week, anyway." He blew out a breath. "I'm attending my franchisor's annual franchisee conference. I was planning to skip this one—until they named me franchisee of the year. I've been waiting for this for more than thirty years. It may not sound like much to you, but it's a very big deal to me."

Tim reached over and clapped Frank on the back. "Congratulations! That's a huge accomplishment."

"It's super that Loretta is on board with your going," Glenn commented.

"She doesn't know." Frank bit his lower lip. "I haven't told her—yet. I've been looking for the right time."

Glenn and Tim stared at him.

"Since I'm already going to San Francisco for an overnight, I can extend my trip by another day or two to help David. I love that kid and am so proud of what he's accomplished. I owe it to him, too. If it hadn't been for me, his dad might still be alive."

"Hold on," Tim said. "You didn't cause William Wheeler to commit suicide. He made that choice on his own."

"Tim's right, Frank. You both got sucked up into something you couldn't control. It got out of hand. His reaction was tragic, to be sure, but you paid a price too. Everyone in Westbury knows you went above and beyond in fulfilling the community service part of your sentence."

"You also paid a huge fine. If you're feeling guilty, you shouldn't be. The way you've conducted yourself has shown everyone that you're a good man, Frank," Tim said.

Frank blinked rapidly.

"If you can help David next week, that would be very kind," Glenn said.

"I'll talk to Loretta about it tonight and let you know," Frank said.

"Great," Glenn replied. "I'm sure Gloria and that posse of gals she runs around with will sweep in with meals and anything else Loretta needs while you're gone."

For the first time since they'd sat down, Frank smiled. "I've been ignoring calls from David, too. I'll swing by his house on my way home tonight to talk to him and his mom. Jackie has to be okay with me going with him, too. Then I'll present it to Loretta."

Glenn signaled to Pete for the check. "This one's on me."

Frank reached for his wallet. "No. Let me..."

Glenn shook his head. "You can pay next time. I think we should make this a regular thing."

Tim nodded his agreement as he scraped up the remaining crumbs of his pie.

CHAPTER 30

*F*rank stepped out of his office before four, turning the light out and shutting the door behind him. "Do you mind locking up, Mary?"

Mary's brows shot up. "Of course not. You're leaving early?"

"I thought I'd surprise my family."

"I'm sure they'll want to celebrate your being named franchisee of the year." Mary beamed as she said the words. "I've never seen anyone work harder. You deserve it."

"I haven't mentioned it to Loretta yet." Frank halted in front of her desk. "Since I have to fly to San Francisco to receive the award, I wanted to talk to Loretta in person."

"I'm sure she'll understand your being away from home." She tapped her computer screen. "You sent me your itinerary —you're only going to be gone one night."

"I'm thinking of extending my stay through the end of the

week. That will mean you'll have to open and close the office every day. I'll check my email and you can call me, but my absence will place an extra burden on you."

"Don't you worry about that." Mary smiled reassuringly. "I can handle things for a few days."

"I know you can," Frank said. "I'm on my way to see someone now. Our conversation will determine whether I prolong my trip. I'll have my answer by tomorrow morning."

Mary nodded. "Have a good night. I'll close the office at five."

"Thank you, Mary. See you in the morning."

Frank made the drive to Forever Friends. He parked in his usual spot behind the building and entered by the back door. The familiar jumbled smells of dogs, cats, and antiseptic cleaners greeted him. A sense of comfort washed over him, as it did every time he walked through that door.

He searched through the premises, looking for David, until he came to the welcome desk.

"David left right after this morning's obedience class," the woman at the desk said. "Did you hear about his mother?"

Frank nodded.

"David won't be in until the day after tomorrow."

Frank turned and retraced his steps, detouring to walk up and down the aisles of kennels. Without exception, every dog and cat came out to greet him. He reached through the wire grates to touch an ear here, stroke a muzzle there, or allow a skittish animal to smell him. He spoke to each one in gentle tones, assuring them they were safe at Forever Friends. Nothing bad would happen to them ever again. People hadn't always seen the good in Frank, but animals recognized it in him. Every time.

He took one last deep gulp of the calming air and went to his car. In another twenty minutes, Frank was standing at David Wheeler's front door.

"Frank!" David threw the door open. "Come in."

"I just heard about your mom." Frank stepped into the tiny entryway. "How is she?"

"Okay. If she stays in bed with her foot up, she's fine," David said. "It hurts to walk."

"I'm really sorry to hear this. Glenn and Tim told me. Will she need surgery next week?"

David shook his head. "The doctor just called. They don't have to operate. They'll put her in a special cast tomorrow. She'll be on crutches for a while."

"That's good. Then you can still go to California next week."

David furrowed his brow. "We're not going—Mom canceled our flights. I just told you, Mom can't walk. I'll have to find a place by looking online."

"That's why I came by to see you, David. I'd like to take you to California. Finding a decent place to live—without actually seeing it or the surrounding area—is pretty iffy."

David did a double take. "But you're so busy with Haynes Enterprises that you work late every night and you never stop by Forever Friends. You don't have time to go to California with me."

"I'm going to San Francisco next week on business. You could come with me—my meeting is only one day and evening—and we could drive across the Golden Gate Bridge to spend a couple of days getting to know San Rafael and finding a place for you to live." He smiled at the boy who he loved like a son. "What do you think?"

"That'd be great!" David raked his hand through his hair. "I can't believe this. I was worried that... well..."

"Things would fall apart and you wouldn't get to follow through on your dreams?"

David looked away and nodded.

"I won't let that happen, David. You've worked too hard to get this job at the Guide Dog Center. I'm excited about opening a guide dog training school at Forever Friends, too. This is a shared vision."

"What do we do now?" David asked.

"We should talk to your mom to make sure she agrees with this plan. Is she up to seeing me?"

David nodded. "She's awake. Mrs. Torres brought us a casserole for our dinner tonight and visited with mom. She just left."

"Good. Let's clear things with her now. I need to talk to Loretta, too. I'll do that tonight, then I'll book flights and hotels for both of us."

David nodded enthusiastically. "I can't believe this, Frank."

"I'm sorry I've been so... out of touch."

David shrugged. "You were busy. I understood."

"We'll get caught up next week," Frank said.

David led Frank down the hallway to his mother's

bedroom. "Mom—Frank's here and he has an idea. Can we come in?"

"Sure," Jackie called in reply.

Frank, Jackie, and David quickly agreed to a plan for the following week.

"If I could get up to hug you, I would," Jackie said. "I can't tell you how much I appreciate this, Frank. You're a Godsend."

David walked Frank to his car with a spring in his step.

Frank hoped Loretta would be as enthusiastic about his planned trip as David and Jackie were.

CHAPTER 31

$\mathcal{T}$im ushered a young couple through the door at Pete's Bistro. At three o'clock on a weekday afternoon, the popular restaurant on the town square was not busy. He saw Pete leaning against the bar, bent over a pile of receipts. Tim motioned with his head toward his favorite booth at the far side of the room.

Pete smiled and gave Tim a thumbs-up, then spoke to a server polishing wine glasses behind the bar.

Tim led his clients to the table. The server joined them.

"Hello, Mr. Knudsen. Taking a break from house hunting?"

"We are. The Parkers are relocating here. From Philadelphia."

"Welcome to Westbury," the server said. "I moved from Chicago two years ago and I love it."

"You don't miss big-city life?" Sherry Parker asked.

"Not a bit. I can do everything I did there, but without the hassle of traffic and congestion. What brings you here?"

"I'm a veterinarian. I'll be joining John and the team at Westbury Animal Hospital," Sherry said.

"John Allen is wonderful," the server said. "He treats my dog and cat. You're going to love it there."

"I hope so," Sherry said. "Neil's just graduated from Wharton and is looking at business opportunities here."

"That's great," the server said.

"We've seen several houses today that fit their needs," Tim said. "We thought we'd take a few minutes to discuss each one." He turned to Sherry and Neil. "Are you hungry?"

They both shook their heads.

"I could use a cup of coffee," Sherry said.

"Me too," Neil chimed in.

"Bring us a pot and three cups," Tim said. "If you've got any of Laura's cookies back there, bring us a plate of those, too."

The server nodded. "I'll make a fresh pot and be right back." The restaurant didn't offer cookies on the menu, but they kept a stash for Tim. He frequently brought clients to the bistro as a respite from house hunting. He usually ordered coffee and always ordered cookies.

Sherry looked around the room. "This is a very comfortable place," she said. "We'd planned to stop in when we came here to interview for my job, but ran out of time."

"Pete's is routinely voted Best Restaurant in Westbury. If

you like a steakhouse, you can't do better than Stuart's Steakhouse. And if pizza is what you're after, look no further than Tomascino's. You'll want to remember Laura's Bakery, too. That's where the cookies you're about to sample are from. Laura and Pete are married."

"Was that her storefront next door?" Neil asked.

"It was."

"It looks like an authentic French patisserie."

"You noticed that?"

Neil nodded. "We drove around the square when we were here before. There's a fine jeweler, a bridal shop, a specialty toy shop, and a high-end gift shop, too."

"You've been paying attention." Tim smiled approvingly.

"I'm trying to decide what sort of business I'd like to open here. I've researched the demographics—gender, age, median household income."

The server poured them each a steaming cup of coffee before leaving the insulated pot, cream and sugar, and a plate of iced sugar cookies on the table.

"Sugar cookies! My favorite," Sherry said, picking up a half-moon-shaped cookie iced to look like a slice of watermelon. She took a bite and moaned. "These are fabulous."

Tim stirred cream into his coffee and took a sip. "What are your conclusions?" he asked Neil.

"Westbury is a well-heeled community. The storefronts and businesses look well-maintained and prosperous. Being home to Highpointe College is a plus, too. Westbury will be a great place to start a business."

"I couldn't agree more. What sort of business are you considering?"

"I'm thinking of a fast-food franchise. I wrote my thesis on that business model. I know it doesn't sound glamorous, but they're virtually recession proof and are easy to scale."

"One of Westbury's most successful business owners is Frank Haynes. He owns fast-food franchises."

Neil nodded. "I know. I found his name in my searches and looked him up. He's even franchisee of the year for one of his brands. Haynes owns several franchises and has cornered the market here in Westbury." He sighed. "If I stick with fast food, I think I'll have to go outside of Westbury."

Sherry finished the watermelon cookie and started in on an iced smiley face.

"Frank's a good friend of mine," Tim said. "Would you like to talk with him?"

"Sure—but I'm not sure he'd want to. I'd be moving into his logical expansion territory."

"I don't think he'd see it that way." Tim pursed his lips. "Frank and his wife just had twins—which makes them parents to five kids. He also owns and operates the no-kill shelter in town."

"Forever Friends." Sherry covered her mouth with her hand. "John told me about it—and Frank's plans to expand it to include a guide dog training school."

"Yes. That's where Frank's real interests lie. I might be mistaken, but I don't think Frank plans to expand his restaurant empire. I'll bet he'd be delighted to meet with you."

"In that case, I'd be grateful if you'd introduce us."

"I'll do just that," Tim said. "And now, let's talk about the houses we saw this morning. Do any of them stand out?"

Sherry and Neil looked at each other and smiled.

Tim knew that smile. They'd made their decision. He felt like he was the real estate agent on that television show where the families decide whether to love their home or list it. "Well... what will it be?"

CHAPTER 32

rank pulled into his garage. He'd been rehearsing, all the way home from David's house, how he'd present his upcoming trip to his wife. He inhaled slowly. Even to his own ears, he hadn't come up with a winning pitch. If he were being honest, he would remind her he was rarely home while the kids were awake, so his absence wouldn't make much difference.

He forced himself to get out of the car. Frank was ten feet from the door into the house when he noticed the jumble of gardening tools sitting in a pile of dirt along the wall. Sean had promised to weed the flower beds, and they'd agreed to increase his allowance.

Frank rubbed his hand on the back of his neck. The disheveled tools stood out like a sore thumb in the otherwise tidy garage. He hung the tools on their hooks, taking care to remove every speck of dirt that still clung to them. Frank then swept up the garden soil on the floor into a dustpan and deposited it into the trash can. He fastened and refastened the lid repeatedly until the door into the house banged open.

"Daddy!" Nicole rushed to his side and threw her arms around Frank's waist. "You're home!"

"Frank?" Loretta called from the kitchen.

Frank hugged Nicole tightly, lifting her feet off the ground.

Nicole squealed with pleasure.

Frank set her down. They entered the house and headed for the kitchen.

"It is you," Loretta said, giving a pot of beans one last stir before placing the spoon on the counter and turning off the burner.

Frank crossed to her and planted a kiss on her forehead.

"You're right on time for dinner," Loretta said. "I can't believe you're here. What's up?"

"Can't a man come home to have dinner with his family?" Frank meant for the rhetorical question to sound funny, but his voice had an edge to it.

Loretta was taking a pork roast from the oven and didn't notice. "Would you call Sean? He's out back, playing with the dogs."

Frank went onto the patio and called to the boy.

"Dad!" Sean dropped the ball he was about to throw for Daisy and raced to the door.

"Mom says it's time for dinner. Go wash your hands."

"Yes, sir." Sean headed for the bathroom.

"Where's Marissa?" Frank asked, returning to the kitchen.

"She and Grace just left for Marissa's dance class. Grace will drop her off and come back here to help get Nicole to bed and then clean up the kitchen while I feed Bonnie and Branson." Loretta stopped spooning a mixed green salad into bowls. "Since you're home, I'll text Grace and tell her she can go home instead of coming back here. Marissa gets a ride home with one of her classmates every night. And Nicole and Sean will be glued to you."

"No. Actually, I…"

Loretta slapped the counter with her palm. "So help me, Frank. You are not going back to work. You can spend an evening with your family for once."

Frank bristled. "I wasn't planning to go back to work."

"Okay. Good. I'm sorry I snapped." She reached for her cell phone and sent the text to Grace.

"I've got something I need to discuss with you."

Loretta resumed portioning out the salad. "We can talk after the kids are in bed."

Frank didn't respond.

Loretta glanced over her shoulder at him. "That's okay, isn't it?"

Frank nodded.

"Will you help me bring the food to the table? I'm starved. I swear, I've been hungry ever since I started nursing the twins. My baby weight is all gone, too. Besides the health benefits for the babies, nursing has peeled the weight off of me. See these jeans I'm wearing?" Loretta ran her hands down her thighs. "These are my pre-pregnancy skinny jeans. They're almost too big!"

Frank cast an appreciative glance at his wife. "You're always gorgeous to me—no matter what you weigh."

Loretta rolled her eyes, but the flush that rose from her collar showed she loved the compliment.

Frank brought the baby swings into the dining room and placed them next to his chair. He placed Bonnie on his left and Branson on his right. They snoozed as the seats carried them forward and back while the family ate dinner.

Frank forced himself to try everything. He loved Loretta's cooking, but couldn't manage more than one bite. He pushed things around on his plate. Frank knew he should be reveling in this family time, but he was anxious about his talk with Loretta.

They finished dinner, and he'd carried his plate to the sink, scraping his food into the disposal before Loretta noticed what he was doing. He read an extra bedtime story to Nicole and watched Sean demonstrate how adept Daisy was at catching a Frisbee. An exhausted Marissa had hit the shower and gone straight to her room after getting home from class. The dishwasher was humming, and the twins had been fed and were asleep. It was time for Frank to broach the subject of his trip with Loretta.

Loretta padded to him on slippered feet. She rested her head on his shoulder and yawned. "If you want to talk to me, you'd better do it now. I'm almost asleep on my feet."

Frank took a step back. "Let's go outside. We can sit on the patio."

"Sure," Loretta said, following him. She sank onto the glider and patted the spot next to her.

Frank sat down stiffly. "I've got something to tell you— and I don't think you're going to like it."

Loretta straightened, now fully alert. "What's that?"

"I've got to go to San Francisco next week. To franchisee headquarters."

"That's the yearly meeting, right?" She pulled her hair off her face. "You told me you weren't attending this year. You said it's no fun to go without me." Her volume increased. "You promised you'd stay here with the kids and me."

Frank turned his face aside. "I have to go."

"Why do you have to go?"

He took a deep breath before continuing. "Because I've been named national franchisee of the year. I've been working for this my entire career. I need to be there to receive the award in person."

"Franchisee of the year?" Loretta leapt to her feet. "That's great, Frank, but you've been telling me—ever since the babies were born—that the business was in trouble. That was your excuse for working late every night." She paced. "That was a lie, wasn't it?" She swung on him. "You're franchisee of the year! The business is doing better than ever."

Frank shrunk back from her.

Loretta continued her tirade. "You stayed away to avoid us, Frank. At a time when we all needed you—you chose not to be here." Her voice cracked, and she started to cry. "I've been so desperately lonely for you. And the kids spend every evening listening for the garage door to tell them you're home before they go to bed. Which you never are."

Loretta pulled a tissue from the pocket of her jeans and

blew her nose. "What is going on with you? Don't you love us anymore?"

Frank got quickly to his feet. "I love you and this family more than ever. I think about how lucky I am to have you every minute of every day."

"You have a strange way of showing it." She turned her back on him.

"There isn't a moment that goes by when I don't realize how unworthy I am of all this." He held his arms wide. "I'm trying to make sure you're all well taken care of. That's something I know how to do."

Loretta looked back at him. "What are you talking about? Unworthy? You're a kind and decent man, Frank. Surely you know that by now."

Frank looked at his hands.

Loretta walked to him and put her hands over his. "You listen to me, Frank Haynes. Your family loves and admires the man that you are. We're proud of you." She snuffled. "And I'm very proud of you for being franchisee of the year."

Frank took a deep breath and forced himself to continue. "There's more. I want to stay in California a couple extra days to help David find a place to live when he moves there next month."

"Grace told me about Jackie when she got here today." Loretta sighed. "It never occurred to me you'd be the one to go to California with him in place of Jackie, but it makes sense."

Frank raised his eyes to hers. "Then you'll be all right with me making the trip?"

Loretta narrowed her eyes. "On one condition, Frank. And listen carefully, because I really mean it."

Frank's eyes opened wide.

"You go to California and you return to us as the old Frank. The one who comes home from work every day to be with his family."

"I'll try."

"There's no trying, Frank. If you don't—if you can't—I want you to go to counseling."

Frank took a step back, shaking his head.

"That's the deal, Frank. Something's bothering you. I know it is. You're not eating, you're irritable and avoiding us, and you've taken on obsessive-compulsive behaviors."

"What are you talking about?"

"I've seen you tidying and straightening things, Frank."

"I've always been a neat freak."

"This is more than that." She squared her shoulders. "Whatever's bothering you is more than you can fix on your own. This feeling of yours that you're not worthy is part of it. I believe you need help—professional help." She took his face in her hands. "If you don't come back to us as the old Frank—and I'll know—promise me you'll see a therapist."

Frank looked into the eyes of the person he trusted most. "I promise."

Loretta pulled him to her and they clung to each other before she finally took his hand and led them to bed.

CHAPTER 33

"Wow! Our rooms are on the thirtieth floor." David turned to Frank as they took the elevator up. "I've never been in a building taller than ten floors."

"I think our rooms are right across the hall from each other. One should have a view of the bay and the other, the city. When we get up there, you can choose which one you'd like."

"Really? That'd be cool."

"I need to attend a meeting this afternoon," Frank said. "If you're hungry, you can order lunch from room service."

"Geez—I've never done that before, either."

"Get what you want," Frank said. "It's on me. And if you want to go outside to explore, make sure you have your cell phone with you. Text me when you leave the hotel and when you get back."

"I don't know. It looks like a very big city to me. Sort of scary."

"There are areas in San Francisco where you definitely don't want to go," Frank said, "but if you stay on the major streets near the hotel, you'll be fine."

The elevator stopped at their floor and they stepped out.

Frank pointed to two sets of numbers fixed to the wall in front of them. "Our rooms are this way." He led them to the right.

"As long as we've found you a place to live, I thought we could come back to San Francisco on Friday morning to do some sightseeing before our flight home at three."

"That would be great."

"We'll cross the Golden Gate Bridge on our way to San Rafael. We can go to Fisherman's Wharf—or the Presidio. Golden Gate Park is also spectacular. I'm sure you'll make friends at the Guide Dog Center and your group will go to all these places. It's a fabulous city. Make sure you enjoy it while you're living so near by."

"I don't think I'd want to come in on my own, but it'd be fun in a group."

Frank stopped in the middle of the hallway. "Here we are." He opened a door and rolled his suitcase into place to hold it open. He then opened the other door. "Other than the view, both rooms are the same. Take your pick."

David stepped into the first room and turned in a circle. "This is like on a TV show."

"It's one of the nicest hotels in the city," Frank replied.

David walked to the window. The street far below was

teaming with cars and the sidewalks were crowded with pedestrians. He turned back to Frank. "It seems so—crowded. There's people everywhere."

"Look at this view." Frank gestured to the window of the other room.

David walked past him and sighed heavily. "The water is beautiful. You can see so far from up here."

"I take it this will be your room?"

David nodded.

Frank wedged David's suitcase into the doorway and joined the teen at the window. "You can't see it from here," he said, "but San Rafael is over that way." He pointed into the distance.

David swallowed hard. "Will it be like San Francisco? All busy and full of people?"

Frank put his hand on the boy's shoulder. "No. San Rafael is much more like Westbury than it is San Francisco. Not nearly as congested."

"That's good. I don't think Dodger or I could stand to live in a place like San Francisco. What do people do with their dogs here? Do they even have dogs?"

"Sure they do." He looked at the boy. "They do what people—and dogs—always do: adjust to their surroundings."

"I'm glad we won't have to."

"Here's your room key," Frank said, handing him what looked like a credit card. "I'm going to put my suitcase in my room and head downstairs to my meeting."

"I'll order lunch and watch TV," David said. "I don't want to go out there on my own."

"I'll check in with you before the awards banquet tonight," Frank said.

"I'll be ready. What time is it?"

Frank cocked his head to one side. "Are you coming with me?"

"Sure! Mom made me pack my church clothes, so I'd be appropriate. I have a tie and everything." David furrowed his brows. "I'm invited, aren't I?"

"Of course you are." Frank blinked rapidly. "I didn't think you'd want to waste time going to a boring business dinner with me, is all."

"I can't wait to hear them call your name, Frank. And see you up on that stage. You're the most successful person in Westbury."

Frank flushed. "I think Maggie Martin deserves that honor."

David shook his head. "I don't agree."

Frank coughed into his elbow. "Well... I'd better get to my meeting. Tonight's dinner starts with a cocktail hour at 6:30. I'll knock on your door at 6:15."

"Sounds good."

Frank walked to the door, then turned back. "Do you know how to order room service?"

David shook his head.

Frank smiled and supplied David with another life lesson.

CHAPTER 34

rank and David sat together at a round table at the front of the ballroom. Frank chatted with the man on his left while David worked his way through a mixed green salad with toasted pine nuts and goat cheese and then quickly consumed his entire filet mignon.

Frank turned to his young companion. "Are you enjoying your dinner?"

"The food here is incredible," David said around a mouthful of whipped garlic mashed potatoes. "You're not eating. Don't you like the food?"

"It's not that," Frank said.

David paused, his fork halfway to his mouth. "Then what is it?"

Frank inhaled slowly. "I'm just nervous about my award, is all. I have to make a speech."

"Like at the Oscars?"

Frank smiled. "Something like that."

"You'll be great." David set his fork into motion again. "You always are." He gathered the last morsels of potato onto his fork and popped it into his mouth.

"I'm not going to eat my entrée," Frank said. "Would you like it?"

David nodded. "Absolutely. If you're sure."

Frank picked up David's newly cleaned plate and put his in its place.

The president of the franchise company took to the podium and started his remarks.

David had polished off Frank's meal by the time the president announced Frank as franchisee of the year.

Polite applause filled the crowded ballroom.

Frank rose and made his way to the stage.

David clapped so hard that his hands stung.

Frank shook the president's hand and accepted a tall, engraved crystal obelisk. He stepped to the microphone and rested the award on the podium. Frank stood, head down, for what seemed like an eternity.

A titter of conversation circled the room.

"Frank," David hissed in a stage whisper.

Frank brought his head up and began to speak. "All of us in this room own fast-food franchises. We feed millions of hungry people every day. I take enormous pride in that. Our meals are wholesome and our ingredients are fresh. Quality control in our industry is superb. When our customers stop at one of our restaurants, they know what to expect. And they know they can afford to feed their families.

"Hunger remains a problem in all of our communities. We"—he swung his arm to include the audience—"are part of the solution to that grievous issue. Because of us, the person who's working two jobs to support a family can get a full meal between shifts. Students know where to go for food they can afford. And families that run from school to extra-curricular activities can have dinner before they get home at the end of a long day."

He looked out at the crowd. "Some in the food industry look down on us and our offerings. I'm here to tell you I'm proud of what I do—of the contribution I make to our community. I hope you are, too." He picked up the obelisk and turned to the company president. "Thank you for this award. I'm deeply grateful."

The room erupted in applause.

David was on his feet, clapping wildly. The other guests at their table joined him.

Frank made his way back to their table, shaking hands extended to him in congratulations. He was stopped, twice, by other attendees who insisted on taking selfies with him.

When he finally took to his seat, the others at his table showered him with praise for his inspiring remarks.

The man to his left put his arm across Frank's shoulders, commenting on how much he appreciated the speech. Frank abruptly shook the man's arm off and stood. He turned to David and opened his mouth to speak, then thought better of it. He pushed back his chair forcefully, almost knocking it to the floor. Frank threw his napkin onto the table and stormed out of the room.

DAVID LOCKED eyes with the startled man who had been talking to Frank. The other faces at the table registered their shock. David got up and wove his way through the tables in pursuit of Frank.

He stopped in the wide hallway outside of the ballroom and looked both ways. Frank was nowhere to be seen. He checked the men's room, calling his name. Frank didn't answer.

David took the elevator to the street level. He surveyed the busy lobby, then hurried out the revolving door and onto the street.

Frank leaned against the wall of a shop, now closed for business, halfway down the block from the hotel.

David hurried to his side.

"Frank—what's going on? Are you okay?"

Frank nodded and turned his face away from David.

"What happened in there?"

Frank shrugged.

"I thought maybe you got sick or something."

Frank didn't answer.

"You scared me, Frank."

"What do you mean? I'm in good health. You know that. There's nothing to be scared of."

David grabbed his arm. "Good health isn't just physical."

Frank lifted his eyes to David's.

"My father committed suicide, remember?"

Frank drew in a quick breath. "I remember. Are you worried…" his voice broke.

"About your mental health? Yes—Frank—I am. You acted crazy back there. Your speech moved the people in that room. I watched their faces. You should have seen them. Everyone in there looks up to you. And then you come back to your seat and act like such a jerk to that guy?"

Frank opened his mouth to speak.

David held up a hand to stop him. "There's more. You never come to Forever Friends—you never answer my texts or emails. And then you step in and take me on this trip. Sean tells me you work all the time. He never sees you. When he asked his mom about it, she told him you had to work late because the business was in trouble—but here you are, winning an award." He stepped back, raking his hands through his hair. "This isn't the Frank I know." His tone was firm. "What is going on?"

"I'm not sure I know anymore. Believe me, I realize how blessed I am: by my family—and I include you in that—by my thriving business and this award, and all the new friends I have in Westbury. I feel like I'm finally living the life I always wanted."

"That's all good stuff."

"Yes—it is." Frank's voice grew anguished. "But it's all built on a lie."

"No, it's not."

"It is! I'm a felon, David." Frank spat the words. "I've done terrible things to people—I've hurt them. Bonnie and

Branson don't know that about me yet, but one day they will. What'll they think of their dad when they find out?"

"You made mistakes, Frank. And you paid for them. Look at all the good you've done for the pension fund and the town."

Frank cradled his head in his hands. "If I hadn't been involved in Delgado's schemes, things wouldn't have gotten so out of hand." He struggled to choke out the next words. "Maybe your dad would still be alive. I'm so sorry, David."

"You both got involved in something you never intended to. Delgado's cronies were experts at pinning things on other people. I know my dad—he wasn't guilty of masterminding that fraud. They framed him." David's voice was hoarse with tears. "I lost my dad to all that shit, Frank. I can't lose you to it, too."

Frank brought his head up.

"You've got to forgive yourself. Everyone else already has. Loretta and the kids need you to be there for them." He took a ragged breath. "Me too."

"I thought I was over feeling like this—until the twins were born. It all came crashing down on me—only ten times worse."

"How did you get over it before? Did you go to counseling?"

"No."

"I did—after dad died. Mom made me, even though I didn't want to. I was furious at dad—and you. The counselor helped me. "

Frank pursed his lips. "That's what Loretta said. She's

been... upset with me, too. I promised I'd go when we got back if I wasn't better."

David swiped under his eyes with the palm of his hand. "You're definitely not better. I think you should go."

Frank studied the boy's face, then nodded. "You're right. I'll go."

"Really?"

Frank nodded. "Yes."

"Great," David replied.

"Are you hungry?" Frank asked. "Silly question. I know you just finished dinner—two dinners, actually." A smile played on his lips.

"I can always eat. You know that," David replied.

"Good, because I'm suddenly ravenous. And that diner at the end of the block," he pointed to the other side of the street, "has the best pork chops in the country."

"Seriously?"

"Do you want to see for yourself?"

"Sure."

Frank drew David to him for a quick hug. "Thank you, son," he said.

David nodded, and the two of them headed to the diner.

CHAPTER 35

$\mathcal{G}$ ordon raised his hand over his head in greeting to the man on the other side of the busy street.

Robert waved back to acknowledge that he'd seen Gordon and waited for the light to change before crossing the street at the end of the block.

Gordon walked up to meet him, extending his hand. "I'm glad you could make it. The brooch is far from the most valuable item I've placed in an auction, but I'm most excited about it."

They turned and walked through the early evening sunshine.

"I love coming to Mayfair every chance I get," Robert said. "It's beautiful, especially in the summer. If I could afford to live here, I would."

Gordon glanced over at his new friend and nodded in agreement.

"I'm really excited about attending this auction. Thank you for inviting me. Is there anything I need to know? I plan to sit on my hands—I don't want to be mistaken for a bidder."

Gordon chuckled. "Don't worry about that. All bidders will have paddles. The auctioneer won't recognize you for a bid if you're simply scratching your nose or adjusting your glasses."

"That's a relief! I looked at the catalog for this auction. I can't afford any of it. Those Cartier pieces sound amazing. And the Harry Winston diamond and emerald necklace. It's hard to believe there are people out there who actually wear those pieces."

"Plenty of them, as it turns out," Gordon said. "Our Van Cleefs & Arpels brooch is one of the more modest items in the auction."

"It's also one of the prettiest," Robert said.

"I agree with that." Gordon stopped underneath a large dark blue flag hanging over a glossy black door set into an imposing stone edifice. The name of the decades-old auction house was emblazoned on the flag in gold letters. He pressed a buzzer at the door.

A uniformed guard let them in. "Hello, sir," the man said to Gordon. "Nice to see you again."

"Thank you," Gordon said. "My colleague and I are here for the seven o'clock auction."

"Of course," the man said. "Sign in and they'll direct you to the auction room."

They crossed the marble floor of the paneled lobby to a

reception desk. A grand staircase of gleaming mahogany swept along the wall opposite the door.

They entered their names in a leather-bound volume. The receptionist asked for their identification and consulted her computer screen. "Yes, gentlemen—here you are. Welcome. You'll be in the auction room on the next floor. The lift is through there"—she pointed to a hallway across from her—"or you can take the stairs."

"Thank you," Gordon said, looking at Robert.

"Let's take the stairs. They've got art hanging all the way up."

Gordon smiled. "Those will be items on display for future auctions. That's one reason I suggested we arrive early. It's fun to stroll around to see what's coming up for sale."

They crossed to the carpeted stairs of the staircase.

"The volute and finials on the balustrade are works of art in themselves," Robert said. "The carving is exquisite."

Gordon's expression showed his satisfaction. "I'm glad you notice such things. This sort of workmanship can't be replicated." He pointed to the crown molding. "The auction house maintains this old building in pristine condition. It's a joy to be here."

They made their way slowly up the stairs, examining a collection of abstract paintings as they ascended. The gallery at the top of the stairs featured a group of modern sculptures.

"This is absolutely fascinating," Robert said.

"Auction houses display items for bidders to examine

before the sale because all items are sold as is. There's no chance to back out once you've made your bid."

"In order to become a bidder—to get a paddle—do you have to furnish proof of your financial ability to pay?"

"Exactly so," Gordon said. "I like to sit in the back of the room, so I can watch all the bidding activity. Do you mind if we find our seats now?"

"Of course not," Robert said.

Gordon led them into the auction room. Rows of white chairs, parted by a central aisle, ran down the center of the high-ceilinged room. The walls were the same rich, deep blue of the flag in front of the building. A pristine white display wall, anchored to a rotating pedestal, sat at the front of the room. The auctioneer's podium was positioned to the left of the pedestal. The auction house's name was tastefully displayed in gold letters on each surface.

A handful of people were already in their seats. The auctioneer was not in the room, but attendants wearing black trousers, white shirts, black ties, and blue aprons embroidered with the company name in gold were stationed at each side of the rotating pedestal. The attendants began pulling on white gloves.

Gordon guided them to seats on the aisle in the back row.

"The people wearing gloves must be the ones showing the item up for bid?" Robert asked.

"Yes. You can't see it from here, but that white wall has hooks for hanging art and will have a stand to display jewelry. There are two sides to the pedestal. While an item is being auctioned, a crew will set up the next item for sale on the other side of the pedestal. The auctioneer keeps things moving along. When the hammer comes down..."

Robert's head swung sharply to Gordon. "They still do that?"

"Oh, yes. When the hammer comes down, the auctioneer will announce the winning bid and the number of the bidder. The pedestal will turn and they'll immediately introduce the next item and start the bidding."

"Sounds very efficient."

"It most certainly is. Auctions are fun to watch—even if you're not bidding. A talented auctioneer has a certain flair—almost a theatricality about them. Their job is to stir up interest and excitement in the crowd. Now that people can view auctions online and bid by phone, that's even harder to do. The auctioneer isn't just working with the people in the room. Our auctioneer tonight is one of my favorites. You'll see him in action."

A steady stream of people entered the room and took seats in the white chairs.

"How does phone bidding work? The auctioneer can't be answering phones."

Gordon pointed to the raised galleries on either side of the room. "That's where the phone bidding takes place."

"They look like large opera boxes," Robert said, "with elevated rows of chairs."

A door that led into the box on their right opened. A tall woman wearing a simple black sheath stepped into the box, clutching a folder to her chest. She walked to the end of the second row of chairs and sat, placing the folder on the narrow table in front of her.

"Who's she?" Robert asked, pointing to the woman.

"She's an employee of the auction house," Gordon said. "Do you see the landline phone on the table in front of her?"

Robert stretched up in his seat. "I can, now. There's a phone on the table in front of every chair."

"That's right. Phone bidders identify the items they're interested in, qualify themselves financially several days before the auction, and are assigned to a representative from the auction house."

"That's fascinating," Robert said.

They watched as the doors into the boxes on either side of the room opened. Men and women, neatly groomed and attired in conservative business fashion, took their seats. The woman in the black sheath leaned across the table to talk to a man who had taken a seat in the row in front of her. He turned to her and made a remark that caused her to shake her head and grin. A man on her left opened his folder and was running his finger down the page, oblivious to the good-natured banter going on around him.

Three representatives in the box on the other side of the room were engaged in animated conversation. One of them tapped at a stack of papers while the other two appeared to be in earnest debate.

"They look like they all know each other," Robert observed.

"They do. They're professionals. They do this here all the

time." Gordon continued his explanation of the process. "The rep calls the bidder a few lots before the item they are interested in, and relays the bidding to them as it takes place. They take direction from the bidder and make bids on their behalf."

Robert narrowed his eyes. "Seems like a lot could go wrong with that."

Gordon nodded. "It does—all the time. A bidder can be on a cell phone and lose their connection. The rep calls them right back—and they're supposed to have one or two backup phone numbers—but that can take precious time. I know of one bidder who lost out on an item he desperately wanted because he drove through a tunnel and lost his connection. His rep wasn't able to restore contact in time."

"If you really want something, it would be best to come to the live auction."

"Some reps may be taking direction from bidders who are on site in a private box, watching the auction live on closed-circuit television. They're VIP customers of the house who don't want their identities known."

"Wow."

"Assigning a rep to a bidder is an art form, too. If a bidder is inclined to be excitable, they're paired with a calm rep. The auction house will match a subdued bidder with a rep who can pump them up. In the end, it's all about getting the best sales price."

All eyes turned to the front of the room as a trim man in a perfectly tailored black suit, black silk shirt, and black tie stepped to the auctioneer's podium. He consulted a stack of papers on the podium, just out of view of the audience, and moved the hammer to the left of the papers.

Conversation in the room ceased.

The auctioneer, his voice amplified by his lapel microphone, welcomed the crowd and laid out the rules concerning payments, taxes, and guarantees.

"Our first item tonight is very fine, indeed," he began, as the turntable swung to the right, revealing two aproned employees standing next to an easel displaying a diamond and emerald bracelet.

"Here we go," Gordon leaned toward Robert and whispered. "Our item is in the fourth grouping."

MAGGIE SWIVELED to her office door and frowned. She'd told Josh she didn't want to be disturbed for the next hour. He was an efficient gatekeeper—this knock on the door had to mean he'd stepped away from his desk.

She turned her laptop away from the door and was getting to her feet when it swung open.

"You're watching it, aren't you?" Susan stood in the doorway. "I was on the way back to my office from the courthouse and decided to stop by. I want to see the auction too. By the time I get back there, the brooch may already be sold."

Maggie nodded and motioned for her daughter to come in.

Susan shut the door behind her.

Maggie quickly retraced her steps to her desk. "I've got it

on my personal laptop. I've rescheduled my calls and meetings for the next hour, so I can see it happen live. They just started." She picked up the laptop and took it to the small conference table in front of the bank of windows overlooking the quadrangle. "I'm not going to get anything done until they've sold the brooch," she said, pulling out a chair. "I'm glad you're here. It'll be more fun to view it with someone else."

Susan sat and scooted her chair close to her mother's. "John couldn't be here?"

"No. He's busy onboarding his new vet."

"That's a good reason. I'm glad he's finally getting some help. He works way too hard."

"I couldn't agree more. Sherry Parker's a real go-getter. They'll make a good team. I'm thrilled," Maggie said.

They watched as the auctioneer coaxed another hundred thousand dollars out of the crowd for a Cartier gold and ruby necklace.

The camera angle switched to a wide view from the back of the room.

Maggie and Susan both leaned toward the screen. "I can't be sure, since we can only see the backs of their heads, but that looks like Gordon and Robert." Maggie tapped the screen to indicate two men on the aisle in the last row.

"Yep. I think you're right."

"And now—a very special piece—with a remarkable mission," the auctioneer said.

"That's us!" Maggie increased the volume.

"This exquisite Van Cleef & Arpels brooch contains over

twenty carats of clear baguette-cut gems lining a double-looped bow, and an arc of marquises surrounding a cluster of round stones in the center. A true statement piece. Proceeds from today's sale will fund the establishment of a seeing eye dog training school in the United States. Every time you wear this lovely piece, you'll be reminded of the life-altering work that you've made possible." He leaned over the podium and spoke as if he were sharing a secret with the crowd. "And I'm delighted to inform you that an anonymous donor has come forward to match today's hammer price with an equal donation to this school."

An excited titter ran through the crowd.

Maggie and Susan turned to each other, eyes wide.

"Who do you think the anonymous donor is?" Susan asked.

Maggie shrugged. "No idea."

"It's not you or John?"

Maggie shook her head. "Frank would be my guess. I'll call him when the auction is over."

"I'll start the bidding at seventy thousand," the auctioneer said.

A paddle went up in the room.

The auctioneer spoke rapidly, increasing the bids in five-thousand-dollar increments at first, before graduating to ten thousand. Paddles raised across the room until the bidding reached two hundred ten thousand.

"I have two hundred ten, for this magnificent piece with the life-changing charitable purpose." He placed his hands on either side of the podium and leaned across it, moving from one side to the other, looking at the crowd in the room and the reps in the box. "Who'll make it two hundred thirty?"

A hand went up in the gallery.

"Thank you, Sarah. Two hundred thirty to you. Who'll give me two hundred fifty?"

A paddle shot up from a man in a white chair in the front.

"And we're two hundred fifty in the room."

A rep from the other gallery bid two hundred eighty thousand.

"Thank you, Duncan. Let's get this into the threes, shall we? Such a good cause." He swung to look at the bidder in the front row and then to Sarah.

Sarah held a hand over her mouth as she spoke rapidly into the receiver of her phone.

"Three hundred, Sarah?"

She gestured with her hand for the auctioneer to give her a minute as she spoke rapidly into the phone.

Maggie and Susan were glued to the screen.

"Any regrets in the room?" The auctioneer spoke to the man in the front row.

Gordon shifted in his chair.

The man held up his paddle.

"And we have three hundred thousand in the room."

Sarah pulled the receiver away from her ear, raised her hand, and called out, "Three hundred fifty thousand."

"And against you, sir. Three hundred fifty." The auctioneer leaned toward the man in the front seat and pointed toward the brooch.

"Fair warning. I'll be selling it now on this side."

The man held up his paddle.

"Three hundred eighty it is." He looked at Sarah. "Such a worthy cause. Let's make it four hundred today, shall we? Think of the lives that will be benefitted—and the matching gift makes it eight hundred thousand."

Sarah was once more covering her mouth and talking rapidly into the phone.

"Fair warning, Sarah," the auctioneer said. "Selling now."

Gordon and Robert leaned forward in their chairs.

"Once more, any other regrets?" The auctioneer scanned the crowd.

Maggie put one hand on her forehead and clutched her chest with the other. "I can't believe this."

"I thought you were hoping to get a hundred thousand," Susan cried.

"Fair warning. Time to sell and move on." The auctioneer stared at Sarah.

Her eyes grew wide as she listened.

The auctioneer reached for the gavel. "Last chance."

Sarah raised her hand. "Five hundred thousand." Her bid soared around the room.

"Five hundred thousand!" He bent over the podium. "To you, sir."

The man in the front row shook his head.

"To the room. Fair warning." He straightened and surveyed the room.

Gordon placed his hand over his heart and rocked back in his chair.

Robert turned to him. "Are you all right, Gordon?"

Gordon's grin matched his answer. "I've never been better."

The auctioneer picked up his hammer and clapped it on the podium with a flourish. "Sold for five hundred thousand to bidder one hundred five." He uncapped a fountain pen and made an entry on a log in front of him.

The podium rotated, a diamond ring designed by Harry Winston came into view, and the process began again.

CHAPTER 36

*D*avid and Frank walked toward their rental car, parked at the curb.

"We've seen all the places with vacancies that I found online," David said. "I need to be close to work so I can come home at lunch to let Dodger out. The only one close enough for that is the first one we looked at."

"The studio apartment?"

David nodded. "It's also the cheapest—and furnished, so that's good."

"It's tiny, especially since Dodger is going to be cooped up there for hours each day."

David's shoulders sagged. "I know. I hate that for him. He's used to having a doggy door out to our big backyard at home."

Frank checked his watch. "It's almost noon. Are you hungry?"

David nodded vigorously.

"Let's get something to eat. We can discuss the options—maybe you can go online and look again?"

"I checked for new listings before we left the hotel this morning." He sighed heavily. "Nothing."

They reached the car.

"You never know—sometimes the thing you're searching for appears out of the blue." Frank slid behind the wheel, and David got into the passenger seat.

"We'll head toward the Guide Dog Center," Frank said. "You'll need to know where to get a meal close to there."

They were soon seated at a small round table outside a sandwich shop in a strip mall. They'd placed their orders at the counter and were waiting for a server to bring their food.

"I can't believe how much our lunch cost," David said, taking a sip of his soda.

"California is an expensive place to live," Frank replied.

"It sure is. I knew apartments cost way more here than in Westbury, but I didn't think about food. I won't be eating out."

Frank looked at the boy he was so fond of and cleared his throat. "About that—I'd like to give you a weekly allowance while you're in training."

"I didn't mean… you don't have to do that. I'll manage. Mom and I made a budget for me, based on what I'll be making. I can do this."

"That's admirable. I'm sure you can, but it's going to be tight. There are always unexpected expenses. I know, from personal experience, how tough life can be when you never have enough."

"You got through it."

"I did—and I don't want that for you." Frank rubbed his chin. "Think of it this way. It'll be a stipend for the first guide dog trainer of Forever Guides."

David smiled. "Okay. You can pay me less when we get Forever Guides up and running."

"We'll see," Frank said as a server placed red plastic baskets containing enormous Italian sub sandwiches, accompanied by long spears of dill pickles and thick-cut potato chips, in front of each of them.

David attacked his sandwich.

Frank took a tentative bite, then another.

A yellow lab in a working harness and wearing a vest printed with the words "Guide Dog in Training" walked past them, her trainer close behind. The dog moved at a fast pace, her eyes focused on the path ahead. She moved to the right to clear their table, ignoring the heady aroma of the sandwiches.

"That's impressive," Frank said. "Sally and Snowball would have stopped and begged."

"Even Dodger would have turned his head," David said. "When guide dogs are working, they can't deviate from the command they're working on."

"I've never seen a guide dog work," Frank said.

David pointed to the sidewalk along the road that bordered the shopping center. "Those people over there are training dogs to cross the street."

They both watched.

"They stop at the curb and the handler tells the dog which way to go. Dogs follow commands."

"What about oncoming traffic? Don't they protect their handler from that?"

"The handler makes sure that there isn't any traffic coming before giving a command to move, but dogs are trained to disobey commands if there's a danger—like a car coming."

The dog and trainer team at the curb crossed the street safely.

"The visually impaired handler uses their ears to assess traffic and dogs use ears and sight," David said.

"How about hybrids and electric cars? You can't hear them—I almost walked in front of an electric car in a parking lot last week. Lucky for me, the driver was paying attention."

"That's a huge problem for the visually impaired," David said. "Some states are considering laws to require vehicles to emit a low-level sound."

"That's a great idea. We'd all be safer."

They finished their sandwiches.

"I'm glad I got to watch guide dogs in training," Frank said. "Pretty soon, you'll be part of one of those teams." He pointed to the dog and trainer, who were continuing to practice crossing the street.

David's face lit up. "I can't wait."

"Let's go take another look at that first studio apartment. Maybe it'll seem better the second time around," Frank said.

Frank was pulling to the curb in front of the building where the studio was located when David leaned forward and tapped the dashboard. "Look," David said. He pointed to a sign in the window of a neat bungalow across the street. "Do you see that?"

Frank squinted and leaned toward the windshield. "It says 'Efficiency for Rent.' "

"What's an efficiency?" David asked.

"It's basically the same thing as a studio apartment."

"That's a house, isn't it?" David asked. "It's got a fenced yard and everything."

Frank and David grinned at each other. "I think we need to find out more about it."

They crossed the street and were climbing the steps to the front door when a voice called to them from the sidewalk.

They turned to see a trim man with a shock of tidy white hair walking a neatly groomed Westie terrier. If the man and dog were to enter one of those contests where the owner looks like their dog, Frank thought they'd certainly be finalists.

"Can I help you?" the man asked as he and the dog climbed the steps to join them.

"We're interested in your efficiency," Frank said, pointing to the sign in the window. "Is it still available?"

"It is. For the two of you?"

"No." Frank introduced himself and David. "David is going to work next month for the Guide Dog Center. He'll be entering the guide dog training program later this year. He needs a place close to the center."

"Ahhh…" The man smiled broadly. "That's a great thing to do. If I were younger, I'd have become a trainer, myself. As it is, I'm a volunteer at the GDC."

"That's cool," David said. "What do you do?"

"I've finally worked my way up the ranks to become a puppy socializer. I spend one morning a week playing with the puppies in the breeding program. It's the best thing I've done in years."

"That does sound ideal," Frank said.

"The efficiency is an apartment behind my garage. There's a small but functional kitchen, a large room with a bed, sofa, desk, and television, and a bathroom with a stacked washer and dryer. Wi-Fi and utilities are included."

"It's furnished?" David sounded hopeful.

"Yep. It may not be the most current style, but it's all solid." He headed down the stairs. "Follow me and I'll show you."

Frank and David grinned at each other behind the man's back.

The apartment was furnished with sturdy maple furniture. Serviceable blinds covered the ample windows. An electric range with coiled burners was impeccably clean, as was the small refrigerator. The place smelled of cleaning products and furniture polish. There was even a doggy door in one wall.

"How much does this cost?" David asked.

The man gave him the figure.

David's shoulders sagged. "That's two hundred more than I can afford. I'm sorry I wasted your time."

Frank was about to speak, but the man beat him to it. "Can you mow the lawn and do yard work?"

"Sure," David said. "I also worked for the best handyman in town back in Westbury—that's where we're from—so I can paint and repair plumbing. I know how to fix all sorts of stuff."

"In that case, I can lower the rent by two hundred."

"Really? That would be awesome. I'll mow and trim, and do whatever you need doing around here. You won't be sorry."

"There's one more thing," Frank said, pointing to the doggy door. "I'm assuming David can bring his dog?"

"As long as it gets along with other dogs." He looked at the Westie sitting patiently by his side. "Dory, here, has the run of the backyard, too. I can't have any issues."

"Dodger is a trained therapy dog," David said. "He gets along with everybody—human, canine, and feline."

"He sounds terrific. We can't wait to meet him, can we, Dory?" He looked down at his companion. "The prior tenant had a dog, and I think Dory is lonesome without her friend."

"Can we sign the lease and pay first and last month's rent now?" Frank asked. "David needs to move in next month. We're here until tomorrow to find him a place to live."

"We sure can. You can cross this off your list of things to do." He extended his hand to David. "My name's Jack Rodriquez."

"Thank you, Mr. Rodriquez."

"Call me Jack."

They made their way to the main house and soon completed the necessary paperwork. Frank furnished the first and last month's rent.

"Welcome. We're looking forward to having you and Dodger as our closest neighbors," Jack said.

Frank and David were getting into the car when Frank's phone began to ring. "It's Maggie," Frank said, his brows drawing together. "She never calls me. I'd better take this."

CHAPTER 37

"Maggie?"

"Frank—I have the most wonderful news." Her voice squeaked with excitement. "Do you have a minute?"

"Of course. I'm in California—with David. We've just found him a place to live."

"That's terrific. Is he there with you?"

"Yes. We just got into the car. He's in the seat next to me."

"Perfect. He should hear this, too. Can you put us on speaker?"

Frank tapped the screen and nodded at David.

"Hi, Maggie," David said.

"I'm so glad I've caught the two of you together." Maggie looked at Susan, who was gesturing at Maggie's phone. "Susan's with me, so I'm going to put my phone on speaker, too. She'll want to hear your reaction."

Susan nodded and grinned.

"Okay. We're all together," Maggie said. "I don't know if you knew, but the auction of the brooch was today—in London."

"I knew it was supposed to be tonight," David said.

"That was London time. They're six hours ahead of us. The auction started about an hour ago and the brooch just went up on the block." Maggie took a deep breath.

"You're killing us here, Maggie," Frank said. "Did it sell?"

"Yes."

"You were hoping to get $100,000. Did it come close to that?" Frank asked.

"No—nowhere near that." Maggie paused again.

"Aww...," David uttered.

Susan narrowed her eyes at her mother and made a rolling hand motion for her to continue.

"We got far more than that. Are you ready for this?" She didn't wait for their obvious reply. "Five hundred thousand!"

Frank gasped, and David whooped. "That's unbelievable. Isn't that far more than the appraised value?" Frank asked.

"It's more than the value of the stones and platinum. Gordon told me that the Van Cleef & Arpels name could skyrocket the amount we'd get. They also announced that the proceeds would benefit the guide dog school. The auctioneer really played that up."

"This is really going to happen, isn't it?" David's voice shook with emotion.

"That was never in doubt, but this infusion of capital will jump-start the process." Frank sucked in a deep breath. "I'm assuming that you're still going to donate the entire amount? That's a lot of money. Maybe you'll want to keep some of it?"

"Of course, we're still going to donate the entire amount." Maggie hurried to reassure them. "But there's even more good news. An anonymous donor has pledged to match the sales proceeds."

Maggie and Susan both leaned toward the phone lying on the table between them, as if trying to get closer to Frank to gauge his reaction.

"What?!" Frank exploded. "That means we'll have one million!" He leaned across the console separating the front seats to hug David.

"Who... who gave the extra money?" David choked out the words.

"That's what we're wondering. Frank—was it you?"

"No. I'd forgotten all about the auction, to be honest, with everything going on in my life right now."

The line was silent.

"Was it you—or John?" Frank asked.

"No."

"Even matching a $100,000 sales price is a lot of money. I'm not sure who that could have been," Frank said.

Maggie raked her hand through her hair. "I've got no idea."

Susan brought her palm to the table. "I think I might know." Her eyes sparkled.

Maggie raised her brows at her daughter.

"Who?" Frank asked.

"If it wasn't either of you—that leaves one more person who's financially committed to Forever Guides."

Maggie's eyes widened. "Of course!"

"Care to fill us in?" Frank asked, his tone bemused.

"Gordon Mortimer," Susan said. "He had agreed to waive his commission, hadn't he?"

"Yes," Maggie replied.

"And he asked me a bunch of questions about the school at that dinner at your house, Maggie. He was really interested," David said.

"It has to be him." Susan leaned back in her chair.

"He talked about how his cousin's guide dog changed his life. Gordon was very moved by their connection." Maggie grinned. "I think you're right."

"I've got to thank him," David said.

"He made the matching donation anonymously," Susan said. "That means he doesn't want his identity to be known."

"But I want him to know…" David began.

"I've got an idea," Frank said. "Forever Guides will have a puppy center for dogs that will be bred for the program and a training center for them when they return from their puppy raisers for formal training. We can name those centers 'Gordon' and 'Mortimer' respectively. Even if he isn't the anonymous donor, he placed the brooch in the auction and waived his commission. I'd like to recognize those contributions."

"Yes!" David cried.

"That's a genius idea, Frank," Maggie said, clasping her hands together.

"I have to agree. I love it," Susan said.

"I can't wait to tell Mom," David said.

"Yes. I need to call John. He'll be over the moon about this."

"Loretta will be, too."

"Okay, everybody. Let's spread the word."

"I'll arrange for a celebration at Forever Friends when we get back," Frank said. "And one more thing, Maggie. Thank you for getting this started by your generous donation of the brooch."

"I think the credit goes to David and Sean," Maggie said. "They found it in that old lost-and-found box at Westbury Animal Hospital."

"In typical Westbury fashion, a whole host of people have come together around a worthy cause," Susan said. "That's one of the best things about living here."

"Amen to that," Frank said. "I'll be in touch when we get home."

CHAPTER 38

"Thanks, Mr. Rodriquez," David said. "I've got plenty of pictures now. My mom was so upset with me last night when I called to tell her I'd found a place to live and I didn't have photos to send her."

"That's very understandable. She wants to make sure you'll be somewhere nice." He smiled at David. "And please call me Jack. If you have any questions before you move in, call me."

"Will do." The three men ambled along the driveway toward the front of the house.

David stopped abruptly and walked over to a hose bib attached to the house. A steady drip of water fell from the spout. He tightened the handle, but the drip continued. "Do you have a wrench I could use?"

"I forgot about that leak. I'll call a plumber."

David scraped at the buildup of hard water deposits. "Let me see if I can fix it for you first."

Jack foraged in the garage and found a wrench.

David finished scraping the residue and employed the wrench. The drip stopped.

"Would you look at that?!" Jack rubbed his hands together. "You're helping out before you even move in." He patted David on the back. "Thank you."

"See you next month," David said. "If you want to, you can make a list of things that need to be repaired, and I'll work on them when I get here."

"I'll do that," Jack said.

"That was a very nice thing you did, David," Frank said as they got into the car. "I'm proud of you."

"It feels good to help people," David said.

"It does." He smiled at the boy. "So—we've found the closest grocery store, drugstore, and Walmart. Anywhere else we need to check out? We've got most of the afternoon left."

"We're near the Guide Dog Center. Do you mind if we drive by?"

"I was hoping you'd say that. It's been fun to see dogs and their trainers around town. They're everywhere. I'd love to see their facility—especially since we're planning to open our own guide dog school when you graduate."

They drove through the wide entrance past a stucco wall where Guide Dog Center was emblazoned in large block letters. A sign directed them to visitor parking. At the end of the lot was a large cargo van, wrapped in photos of adorable puppies, bearing the Guide Dog Center name and logo.

They walked along the landscaped sidewalk to the double glass doors of the entrance.

Frank whistled softly. "This is very impressive," he said. "From what I can see, they probably have seven or eight acres—maybe more."

"When blind people get matched with a dog, they stay here—on campus—for three weeks to train with their dog. I've read reviews of the experience, and many of them mention they feel like they've been at a resort."

"I can see why," Frank said.

They entered the lobby and asked the receptionist about taking a tour.

"You're in luck. There's one leaving in five minutes and we have room for two more." She signed them up and directed them to walk through another set of double glass doors to a courtyard. They joined the small group waiting for the tour.

A thirty-something woman with cropped dark hair approached them with a friendly smile. She introduced herself as one of the administrative staff and invited them to follow her.

Their first stop took them to the puppy building. She opened a large metal door wrapped in a photo of a golden retriever puppy. The spotlessly clean interior contained a birthing center, nursery, veterinarian center, kennels, and a large indoor playroom connected to an outdoor exercise area.

The playroom contained more than a dozen puppies. They were being cuddled, played with, and tended to by a handful of smiling people wearing shirts that announced they were volunteers.

The tour group watched the antics of the puppies through floor-to-ceiling windows, looking into the space. The puppies chased each other, raced up and down training stairs, and rolled around with each other when they weren't being showered with affection by the humans in their midst.

"This must be where Jack volunteers," David said.

"I can see why he loves it," Frank replied.

Their guide explained the breeding program that focused on Labrador retrievers, golden retrievers, and crosses between the two breeds. "The combination of intelligence, temperament, and stamina is crucial for a guide dog. We pull out animals at risk of developing hip dysplasia, which would shorten their working life. Most guides are in service for eight to ten years, so we don't want to cut that short."

A hand shot up.

The guide nodded at the man.

"How much does it cost to train a guide dog?"

"Between fifty and sixty thousand."

A surprised murmur rippled through the crowd.

"That's a lot for someone to pay," he said.

"We don't charge for our dogs," the tour guide said. "Once you qualify, the dog is free. We also provide medical care for the life of the dog. The only thing the owner has to pay for is food and housing. Since they're already living somewhere, housing doesn't cost them anything extra."

She told the group that when the puppies are eight weeks old, they go into private homes to learn basic obedience and become socialized to people and other pets and then they return to the Guide Dog Center campus for formal training when they're fifteen months old.

"I don't think I could do that," a woman said. "I couldn't give up a dog I'd cared for and loved for that long."

"Many people believe puppy raising is a calling," the tour guide said. "We have one woman in our program who has been raising puppies for over twenty-five years. She says she has a puppy to love, not a dog to keep."

"That's an admirable thing to do," another man said.

The tour guide led them to the kennels for the dogs in training. "They're all out working right now," she said. "As you can see, their kennels are large and they have a play yard full of toys."

The next stop was the dormitory for people who came to campus to train with their guide dog. "We're between sessions right now, so you can see the rooms." She opened a door, and turned to the group. "Luxurious, right?"

The group nodded.

"The sidewalk around the dormitory is outfitted with obstacles, changes in terrain, and challenges that the team of dog and handler will face when they're in the outside world. We train them in the basics, here."

"Our last stop will be the gift shop," she said. "Before I leave you there, does anyone have any other questions?"

"You told us that seventy percent of dogs make it all the

way through formal training to become guide dogs. What happens to the rest of them?"

"Great question. Even if a dog doesn't become a guide, it's still a highly trained dog. Many of them go into other service areas. Dogs use scent to help with diabetes management or cancer detection. There are PTSD and trauma therapy dogs, stability dogs, and dogs that help people in wheelchairs. There's a vast universe of needs that trained dogs can help with."

"Do you ever take strays into your program?"

"We don't. Most guide dogs come from a breeding program. Strays can be trained to do some of the other jobs I just mentioned. The California Department of Corrections has a program that pairs up strays with qualifying inmates. Inmates care for and train the dogs as diabetes dogs, first responder canines, and to perform other scent detection tasks. The inmates help the dogs, and the human-canine bond rehabilitates the inmate. It's a win-win situation."

Frank's head snapped up. This prison program appealed to him in a way few ideas had. His own relationship with dogs had helped Frank develop his best qualities. After seeing the Guide Dog Center's facility and operation, he knew it would be years before he could establish something similar in Westbury. Forever Friends, however, had no shortage of strays. Starting a similar canine training program in the prison system back home was something he could easily organize and make happen.

"Do you want to get T-shirts to take home for your family?" David turned back to Frank and found him beaming. He furrowed his brows as he looked at his older friend. David then grinned, too. "You're going to start a prison/canine program like that, aren't you?"

Frank nodded. "Let's get those T-shirts. We can talk about it over dinner."

CHAPTER 39

Frank drove directly home after dropping off David when they returned to Westbury. He was eager to see his family—especially Loretta. He entered the house and received an effusive greeting from Sally, Snowball, and Daisy. Frank bent and patted them in turn, telling them they were good dogs until they quieted down.

He listened for sounds of his family, but heard none. It was dinnertime—the house should be full of noise and activity. The stillness alarmed him. Was something wrong? He lengthened his stride as he headed into the kitchen.

Loretta stood at the counter, tossing a salad. Her long blonde hair hung glossy and straight to her shoulders. She wore a flowered dress that was one of her favorites.

"You're home," she said, smiling at him as she worked. Her lips were pink with lip gloss and mascara darkened her long lashes.

He crossed the kitchen and took her in his arms, kissing her gently.

She circled his waist with her arms and leaned into him.

Frank pressed kisses along her temple, breathing in the citrusy smell of her shampoo. "You look beautiful," he said. "I missed you in San Francisco."

"I want to hear all about your trip," she said, pulling back from him. "You can tell me about it over dinner. It's almost ready." She grasped the salad tongs and placed a serving on each of two plates.

"Where are the kids? Aren't they eating with us?"

Loretta shook her head, and a satisfied smile settled on her lips. "Bonnie and Branson are here, of course, but the other three are spending the night at Susan's."

Frank arched a brow.

"They're all going on a picnic tomorrow along the Shawnee River. The kids are super excited." She opened the oven door and checked their entrée. "These need another few minutes."

"What are we having?"

"Stuffed Cornish game hens." Her voice held a note of pride. "I remember how much you like them."

"I do. That's incredibly nice of you. I can't believe you had the time."

Loretta shrugged. "Gloria may have come over to help me."

"Thank you for going to all this trouble."

"I'm very proud of you. I wanted to celebrate my husband being franchisee of the year."

Frank turned his face aside. "You're so generous, Loretta —especially since I did that while I was ignoring my duties here at home."

She stepped in front of him, and they locked eyes.

"I did a lot of thinking while I was away," Frank said.

Loretta inhaled deeply. "I want to hear all about that, too."

"Can I go see the twins before we sit down to eat?"

"They're snoozing in their swings," Loretta said. "I fed them about an hour ago, so we should have plenty of time to eat and talk before we have to feed them again. You go and I'll bring the salads to the table."

Frank walked to the swings and watched the peaceful faces of his sleeping children. "Your old man's home," he whispered. "I'm going to be better. I'm not there yet, but I'll work on it. I'll be here for you and the rest of the family."

"Ready?" Loretta asked from the doorway into the dining room.

The table was set for two. An array of tapers and votives created a romantic tablescape.

Frank held Loretta's chair for her.

"Fancy," she teased as she took her seat.

"Considering everything you've done, it's the least I could do. I wish I'd have known—I would have stopped for flowers."

Loretta reached over and squeezed his hand. "I'm just glad that you're here." She held his gaze. "Something's changed with you, hasn't it?"

He nodded slowly.

She released his hand and picked up her fork. A smile played behind her lips as she took a bite of her salad.

"It all started at the awards dinner." Frank launched into his story.

"It sounds like you gave a wonderful speech. You must have felt so—I don't know—out of control to have stormed out of a room of people congratulating you."

"That's exactly how I felt. I was embarrassed and ashamed, too, to have acted like that in front of David."

"The fact that he rushed after you shows how much he cares for you," Loretta observed.

"Knowing that boy," Frank's voice cracked, "has been one of the best things in my life. Our conversation—knowing how he feels about me and his dad—helped me more than I can say."

"You've been a blessing to him, too. Look at what Dodger —and his involvement at Forever Friends—has done for him. They've changed the course of his life. You made that possible."

"I keep pushing away the good things I've done to focus on my mistakes." Frank looked at the table. "I need to change that."

Loretta nodded as she picked up their salad plates. "Can you take the hens out of the oven while I put these in the dishwasher?"

Frank followed her to the kitchen. "David made me see what you've been trying to tell me." He removed the pan from the oven and set it on the stovetop. "I can't handle whatever it is that I'm going through on my own."

Loretta served the entrées, spooning sauce over the stuffed hens. She removed a dish of steamed green beans from the microwave and added some to their plates.

"I realized a lot about myself on the trip," Frank said, "and I know I need professional help. All my mental turmoil is affecting me physically, too. Like my not eating." He set the plates on the table. "What's up with that? Have you ever known me to skip a meal?"

Loretta grinned at him. "You've always been able to eat like a horse—and never gain a pound. It's not fair," she chided him.

"I'm going to make an appointment with a counselor. David really liked his, so I'll start there."

Loretta's eyes were moist, and she blinked rapidly. "I'm thrilled. I could tell that you were getting more and more miserable, and I couldn't seem to reach you."

Frank put this fork down and took her hands into his. "I'm so sorry I put you through that. You have enough on your plate."

"None of that matters now. You're going to get help and you're going to get better." Loretta squeezed and released his hands.

"I promise I'll follow through," Frank said. He picked up his knife and sliced off a portion of the hen. "This is delicious," he said around a mouthful. "What did you think about the money raised by the auction?"

"We're all amazed! Everyone in town is talking about it." She leaned back in her chair. "I'm so happy about it, Frank, but I'm also worried."

He tilted his head to one side. "Worried? Why?"

"You're already working eighty hours a week. Starting a new business like a guide dog training school will take even more of your time."

"I've been thinking about it. I can't do that to you and the kids. I have to be home more. End of story."

"I'm glad to hear it," Loretta said. "Maybe you can let someone else handle the creation of Forever Guides?"

Frank pursed his lips.

"You love the shelter and the idea of this new school, don't you?"

"I do. I'm far more interested in them than running Haynes Enterprises. I've done that for so many years that I'm ready for something new. The only problem is, there's no one else to step in and take over the franchise business. And —let's face it—the restaurants bring in all the money."

"Is Mary learning the ropes?"

"She is, but she doesn't have the skills to take over from me."

"Maybe I could come back to work?"

"Do you want to?" He reached across the table to rest his hand on her cheek.

Loretta looked into his eyes and shook her head slowly. "I want to be here with the kids."

"Then that's what you'll do. Let me tackle this problem. I'll talk to my counselor about it, too."

Loretta served them each a scoop of their favorite mint chocolate chip ice cream for dessert. They finished their meal and went to check on the twins.

They stood in front of the swings, arm in arm, watching the miracles they had created.

"I think we've got at least half an hour before they'll stir," Loretta said, turning into Frank and pressing herself against him.

Frank drew her close, and they kissed, their yearning for each other exploding in intensity.

Loretta took Frank's hand and led him down the hall to their bedroom.

CHAPTER 40

$\mathcal{M}$aggie hoisted her carry-on from the top shelf of her closet and brought it to the bed. She was unzipping the empty suitcase when Roman and Eve rounded the corner into the bedroom, followed closely by John.

The dogs stopped short when they saw what lay open on the bed.

"What's this? You're leaving me?" John quipped.

Maggie rolled her eyes at him. "Never."

"I'm going to Chicago for the day. I'll only be gone one night," she said to John. She turned to the dogs. "It's just me. Daddy's staying here."

They seemed to understand and curled up in their baskets on either side of the bed.

"Did I forget you were going?" John's brows drew together in a puzzled frown.

"Nope. This just came up. I was talking to Ian Lawry while you were taking the dogs out."

"The former president of Highpointe?"

"Yes. He's a presenter at this year's Conference of Independent Colleges and Universities. Ian's speaking on remaining active within the higher-education community after retirement."

"Oh… I've never heard you mention the organization. Is this conference going on now?"

Maggie nodded. "I went every year when Paul was president of Windsor College. They have a terrific program for spouses of college presidents. I used to love it."

"But you didn't plan to attend this year?"

Maggie moved to the dresser and began removing a pair of pajamas from a drawer. "I thought about going. The sessions for college presidents are first-rate, too." She placed the garment in the suitcase and paused. "Attending as a college president rather than a spouse seemed… I don't know… awkward. Especially since Paul embezzled from Windsor."

"You weren't part of that." John reminded her. "Besides, you settled with the college for the substantial amount of his life insurance policy. No one knows what Paul did except you and the trustees of Windsor."

"I guess you're right."

"There's no need to hide away, tail between your legs." He caught her eye and she smiled. "Did Ian notice you weren't there and convince you to come?"

"Not exactly. One of his favorite colleagues is chairing a

panel discussion tomorrow afternoon on innovations to attract enrollment. One of the panel participants has had a family emergency and left early. Ian gave his colleague my name. I'm going to fly to Chicago first thing in the morning to join the panel."

"Wow," John said. "That's quite an honor to be asked. Good for you! What will you talk about?"

"I'll basically be giving the same speech I gave our trustees last month—the one on the extra support that working adult students need. Stuff like zoom classes and 24/7 IT support."

"I remember you told me that enrollment of students already in the workforce tripled last year."

"I'll have time to run through my slides and modify them on the plane. I'm slated for a twenty-minute presentation, followed by ten minutes for questions."

"You'll knock their socks off," John said, turning back the covers on his side of the bed.

Maggie went to her closet and returned with a pair of shoes, slacks, a dress, a jacket, and a sweater. "This should do it for now. I'll pack my toiletries in the morning." She placed the items in the suitcase and moved it to the floor before sliding into bed next to John.

"I need to leave here by five. Will you make sure I'm up when you leave for your morning surgeries?"

He put his arm across her and pulled her close. "Sure. When will you get back?"

"The panel is from 2:00 to 4:00. I'll have dinner with Ian and his wife tomorrow night and then fly home on Saturday morning. I don't want to miss the celebration that Frank's got planned at Forever Friends on Saturday evening."

"I think I can survive one night without you," John murmured into her ear. "I'm just glad it's not more than that."

Maggie nestled herself against the comforting form of her husband. "Me, too," she said. "Me, too."

MAGGIE LISTENED INTENTLY to the presentation of the person who preceded her on the panel. His talk on using data-informed insights to guide students through the academic journey was fascinating. If all the sessions were this good, she had been missing out on valuable information. She'd be sure to attend next year's conference.

Her gaze traveled over the attendees in the crowded meeting room. They were packed in at tables arranged classroom-style that stretched to the back of the room. She sat on a raised platform in front with the moderator and her fellow panelists. All eyes were focused on the man standing at the lectern. *I hope my presentation will be as riveting,* she thought nervously.

Maggie's eyes returned to the back of the room. A stately woman in a tailored black suit, white silk blouse, and pearls opened the door and slipped into the room. She slid to her left and leaned against the back wall, next to the three other people who had elected to attend the panel despite all seats being taken.

The woman's eyes found Maggie's and their gazes locked. Maggie shifted in her chair. Was there something familiar about this woman? Perhaps they'd met at an earlier conference. Did she know her? That was ridiculous, Maggie told herself. People attended this conference from all over the country.

Maggie continued to wonder how she knew this woman as the audience clapped and the presenter took his seat.

The moderator read her bio and introduced her, thanking Maggie for making the trip from Westbury to fill the last-minute vacancy.

She rose and took the podium. The woman's gaze from the back wall never wavered. An involuntary shiver ran down Maggie's spine. Was she imagining things, or was there a malevolent look in her eyes?

Maggie opened her laptop, pulled up her first slide, and began her presentation. Her discomfort dissipated as she made her way through her talk. The audience was as attentive to her as they had been to her predecessor.

She concluded her remarks and fielded questions from the audience. The number of hands that shot up when she finished an answer told her the crowd was genuinely interested in her topic. She relaxed as her time ran out and the moderator rose from his seat to thank her and introduce the last presenter.

The woman in the back took a step away from the wall and waved her hand over her head. "I have a question for Mrs. Martin," she called out.

Maggie and the moderator looked at her.

"I suppose we have time for one more," the moderator said as he reached the lectern.

"Isn't it important for a college to be financially sound—in order to attract enrollment?" the woman asked in malicious tones.

Maggie stiffened.

"I'm sorry," the moderator leaned into the microphone. "The session on college finance is down the hall."

"The person who can talk about embezzlement—and its effect on a college—is here, not down the hall."

The room grew quiet. All eyes turned to the woman in the back.

"Or—better yet—tell us how to cover it up."

Maggie felt bile rise in the back of her throat. Now she recognized the woman. She was the wife of a college president from a competing institution within the recruiting area of Windsor. They'd both attended many previous presidential wives' programs at this conference. Maggie had tried to befriend the woman, with no success. Her every overture had been met with a frigid response. And now the woman was here—in the back of the room—intent on harassing Maggie.

Maggie swallowed hard. Colleges were gossipy places. She had been constantly on edge the first few years after Paul's death, waiting for his crimes to come to light. That nothing had surfaced for so long had led her into a false sense of security. It seemed, now, that her reprieve was over.

The moderator spoke. "It's time to move on to our final panelist. Let's give Ms. Martin a round of applause."

The attendees swung back to face the panel and clapped politely.

Maggie took her seat, hoping her burning cheeks didn't look as red as they felt.

The woman in the back gave Maggie a last, withering look, and slipped out the door.

MAGGIE SAT on the edge of the bed when she got back to her room and toed off her pumps. She'd answered the questions of several people who came up to her after the panel concluded. Everyone had been cordial—no one seemed to have noticed or have any interest in the questions posed by the woman in the black suit. Maybe she was making too much of the encounter?

She pulled her phone from her purse and checked her messages. There were two missed calls and a text from Ian Lawry. Maggie frowned as she opened the text.

> My friend told me what happened. We
> can talk over dinner.

Dinner. Maggie bit her lip. She'd forgotten that she was meeting Ian and his wife in the hotel dining room at seven.

She quickly typed.

> Have a headache. Do you mind if I
> take a rain check?

She pressed send.

You can't hide. That'll only fuel the fire
and make things worse.

Fuel the fire?!

Just an expression. Things aren't bad.
The point is to keep it that way. Come
to dinner.

OK

C U in 15

Maggie took a deep breath and got to her feet. She went to the closet and changed into the perfectly cut, deep blue cocktail dress that she'd bought at an end-of-the-season sale the prior year. She hadn't worn it yet, and tonight was the perfect occasion. If people were going to be pointing at her and gossiping behind her back, she was going to look great.

She walked to the entrance of the restaurant at seven on the dot.

"Your party is waiting for you," the host said, taking her to a table in the center front of the restaurant.

Ian and his wife greeted her warmly.

"You look sensational," Mrs. Lawry said.

"Thank you. I'm not feeling too great after this afternoon."

"You're putting on a good face," she replied. "Ian's told me everything."

Maggie nodded. "Good." She turned to him.

"Did you disclose everything to us when we were considering you for the Highpointe presidency?"

"Yes."

"Nothing omitted?"

"I told you everything. Paul and I were living very separate lives by then. I didn't know he was embezzling money from Windsor to support a second family in Scottsdale. None of the stolen funds flowed through our joint accounts. I handled our family finances, and I would have noticed. I didn't even know he owned Rosemont."

Ian nodded. "Then you're in the clear. My advice—ignore this and it will blow over."

"I think I know who tried to upset you today," Mrs. Lawry said. "Was she wearing a black suit, white silk blouse, and pearls?"

Maggie nodded.

"I've seen her at these conferences for years. Most unfriendly and unpleasant. The rest of us long-term presidential wives are quite chummy. Not her. She keeps to herself. I'm not surprised she's the one who took a potshot at you."

"She succeeded in upsetting me," Maggie replied with a wry smile.

"You know what they say," Mrs. Lawry continued. "Haters gonna hate. I think Ian is right. Forget about her. Everyone else has."

Maggie glanced around the room. She really hoped so.

CHAPTER 41

"Hi Ingrid," Frank said as he entered the kitchen.

"Mr. Haynes." Ingrid looked up from the sandwiches she was assembling for the older children's lunches. "It's nice to see you."

"I was hoping to take my beautiful wife to lunch," he replied, looking over his shoulder into the bedroom hallway.

"She's giving Branson a bath," Ingrid replied, slicing the last of three sandwiches on the diagonal and putting it on a plate. "I think that's a wonderful idea. I'm sure she'd love to get out of the house. If you wouldn't mind telling the kids that their lunch is ready, I'll take over for Loretta."

"They're in their rooms?" Frank asked.

"Marissa is. Sean and Nicole are outside with the dogs."

They each headed in opposite directions.

Loretta caught up with Frank in the backyard. He and

Nicole were working Sally and Snowball in the sit command while Sean and Daisy demonstrated.

Sally stood looking at Frank and wagging her tail. She did not sit.

"What is it they say about old dogs and new tricks?" Frank shook his head. "I'm afraid we're a lost cause," he said to Sean.

"She sits for me," Sean said. "You need to work with her."

"I will. I promise," Frank said. He handed Sally's leash to Sean. "I want to take your mom to lunch now, but we can practice again tonight after dinner."

"You'll be home?" Sean sounded skeptical.

"Yes. I'm not going to work late anymore."

Loretta, Sean, and Nicole all stared at him with skeptical expressions.

Frank took Loretta's hand. "Do you have time to grab lunch?"

Loretta nodded.

"We'll be back in a couple of hours," Frank told Sean and Nicole. He glanced between the children and their dogs. "Keep up the good work."

"This is a nice surprise," Loretta said as they walked to his car. "To what do I owe this unexpected pleasure?"

Frank opened her car door for her. "I had my counseling session this morning."

"Your second one. I know."

"It was really great. So helpful. We came up with ideas that I want to discuss with you." He backed out of the driveway. "I didn't want to wait until tonight after the kids are in bed."

"That's wonderful, Frank. I'm excited to hear everything."

"Do you mind if we go to The Mill?"

Loretta looked down at her jeans and T-shirt. "I'm not dressed for The Mill."

"Nonsense. You look gorgeous, and it's just lunch. I want to take you somewhere special, and Pete's is so busy at lunchtime. I want us to relax."

"That sounds lovely."

"I'm hoping we have something to celebrate."

"Gosh—now I'm really curious." Loretta looked at his face in profile as he concentrated on the road. "What did you learn about yourself this morning?"

"For starters, she thinks I'm suffering from postpartum depression."

"What?" Loretta jerked against the seatback and looked at Frank in amazement. "That's not a male thing. Mothers have postpartum."

"Apparently, fathers can get it, too."

"Seriously? I've never experienced it—thank God—but I've had several friends who have. It's horrible for new mothers. All of them had long bouts of crying, too. Have you?"

Frank shook his head. "Everyone doesn't cry. My counselor said that more than ten percent of men suffer from it. That's why I lost my appetite. It explains my obsessive-compulsive behaviors, too."

Loretta's eyes widened.

"All of that was postpartum. Stressing myself out at work by putting in those long hours made it worse, too."

"I had no idea fathers got it!" Loretta raised her hands, palms up.

"It's largely undiagnosed. Men underreport their symptoms and don't seek treatment."

"What does your counselor recommend to help?"

"Several things. For right now, I'm going to stay in counseling. I'm working through the guilt I feel over my part in the fraud and embezzlement from the town."

"You paid that huge fine and worked at least double the community service hours required, Frank. Wasn't that enough?"

"Legally, yes, but not emotionally for me. I've been feeling very guilty that I never served time behind bars."

"I'm glad for that, Frank!"

"I am, too," Frank said. "But I still feel guilty."

He pulled into the parking lot at The Mill and they went inside the historic restaurant on the banks of the Shawnee River.

The maître d' showed them to a table by the window and handed them leather-bound menus. Except for two tables on the other side of the room, they had the restaurant to themselves. The river outside the window snaked in and out of the trees like a golden ribbon circling an emerald-green package.

Loretta inhaled deeply. "So peaceful. I love this view."

Frank drank in the sight of his wife. "I do, too."

Their server approached and cleared his throat. "Would you like a moment?"

Loretta shook her head. "We'd better order. Is there a special?"

The server described a kale salad with chicken, goat cheese, figs, and strawberries.

"I'll have that. And water's fine," Loretta said.

"Same for me." Frank said, handing the server their menus.

Loretta raised her brows. "You're ordering a salad?"

"I'm a new man, remember? The therapist said that nutrition is important. She gave me a handout about diet—it's in the car. I haven't had time to read it yet, but I figure kale is always a good choice."

Loretta grinned. "You *are* making changes."

"That's why I won't be working late anymore."

"Your business is so successful. I thought that being there made you feel better," Loretta said.

"It used to, but not anymore. We talked in therapy about what does make me happy—what gives me life."

"And?"

"You and I discussed this the other night. The things I love most are my charitable enterprises. I'd like to launch a pilot program between Forever Friends and the prison system. Prisoners are carefully chosen to train strays to become various types of service dogs."

"Isn't that what you'll be doing with Forever Guides?"

"Forever Guides will deal exclusively with seeing eye dogs. The training they receive is at a much higher level. I'll pattern my prison program after one in California that's extremely successful."

"That sounds wonderful, but how are you going to juggle a new program, starting up Forever Guides now that you have the money to do so, and run your business?"

The server put their salads on the table.

"That's one of the things I want to discuss with you."

Loretta picked up her fork and nibbled at her salad.

"Do you remember the meeting Tim Knudsen set up between me and Neil Parker?"

"He's the husband of the new vet in town?"

Frank nodded as he speared a large forkful of salad and put it in his mouth.

"I remember you told me you were going to have coffee with him as a favor to Tim."

Frank chewed vigorously and swallowed, washing the greens down with a swig of water. "Eating a kale salad is almost an aerobic exercise," he quipped.

Loretta chuckled. "Maybe take a smaller bite."

"Duly noted." Frank dabbed his lips with his napkin. "It turns out Tim was doing me a favor. Neil and I have met several times. He's as sharp as a tack. And we get along. I've contacted his references and everything checks out."

Loretta cocked her head to one side. "Are you thinking of hiring him?"

"I wanted to run it by you first. I value your opinion." He set his fork on the edge of his plate and leaned toward her. "I'd like him to become my chief operating officer. I'll turn over the daily operation of Haynes Enterprises to Neil."

"Wow." Loretta's eyes widened. "I never thought I'd hear you say that."

"I can expand into the empty office suite next to us so Neil and I will work side-by-side. I'll focus on this new prison partnership and I'll get Forever Guides up and running. If Neil has questions, I'll be available."

Loretta reached for his hand. "You'd be comfortable with this? Do you think you can really let Neil manage Haynes Enterprises without micromanaging him?"

Frank laughed. "I may need to stay in counseling to learn how to relinquish control, but—yes. I want to restructure my life and reorder my priorities."

Their clasped hands rested on the table.

"Then that's what you should do, Frank." Loretta's eyes shone. "I'm thrilled. You have my full support."

"Thank you, darling. I'd like to offer Neil the job this afternoon, but I wanted to talk to you first. If you thought it was a mistake, I wouldn't have done it."

"I think it's the best idea you've had in years!"

Frank squeezed her hands before releasing them. He signaled to the server. "Let's celebrate with dessert."

"That's another terrific idea." Their smiles reached into each other's souls.

CHAPTER 42

$\mathcal{T}$he parking lot of Forever Friends was full at 7 p.m. on Saturday night. The no-kill shelter had closed an hour early—at 4 p.m.—to allow the lobby to be cleaned and caterers to set up beverage and dessert stations. A large sheet cake dominated a central table. Icing outlined a silhouette of a person walking with a guide dog in harness and the words "Thank You, Maggie & John" were written on the cake. A balloon arch in shades of cream, black, gold, and brown loomed over the entrance.

John took Maggie's hand as they approached the door. "You seem a bit… subdued. Are you feeling all right?"

Maggie shrugged. "I'm okay."

"You were so excited for tonight before you went to that conference. Did something happen there?"

Maggie stopped walking and pulled him with her off the sidewalk. "I was going to wait until we got home to tell you."

John raised his brows. "Now I'm really curious."

Maggie gave him a quick recap of her encounter with the woman at the conference.

John ran his hand along her arm. "I think Ian's right. You don't have anything to worry about. Whatever that was—it's blown over."

Maggie looked into his eyes. "You really think I should forget about it?"

"I do."

Maggie nodded. "I'll try."

They made their way into the building and ran into Sam and Joan inside the door.

"This is quite the shindig," Sam said, sipping a soda. "If you'd have told me, all those years ago when we first met at Rosemont, that we'd be here celebrating with Frank, I wouldn't have believed you."

"Lots of things have changed for the better," Joan said. "Best to leave the past in the past."

Maggie and John exchanged a glance. She hoped Paul's past would stay forgotten.

Tonya and George Holmes stepped through the door and joined them.

"Look at this turnout," Tonya said.

"I think Frank invited the whole town," John said.

"And they all came." Tonya smiled. "I'm glad."

Frank appeared from the doorway to the kennels, followed by David. He picked up a glass and tapped it with a knife to get everyone's attention.

The amiable conversation in the lobby petered out.

"Thank you, all, for coming tonight. As you know, I've got a lot to celebrate." He pointed to Loretta, who was standing along the wall behind a double stroller. "First—and foremost —I want to thank my remarkable wife for giving birth to the most beautiful babies in the world. Thankfully, they take after their mother."

The crowd chuckled.

Loretta blushed.

"Forever Friends has a lot to celebrate, too. As you know, David Wheeler is moving to California next week to enter the apprenticeship program at the Guide Dog Center. He'll go to college and learn to become a seeing eye dog trainer. When he's done, he'll come back here to start a guide dog school in Westbury." Frank turned to David. "Will you say a few words about your dream for the school?"

Jackie Wheeler, her foot in an orthopedic boot, sat in a chair next to David. She patted his arm, encouraging him forward.

"Ah… well…" David wrung his hands until he caught sight of Glenn Vaughn.

The older man winked and nodded reassuringly.

David pressed his shoulders back. "Visiting hospitals and care centers with my therapy dog, Dodger," he patted the head of the dog who was never away from his side, "taught me about the miraculous powers of dogs." David gave a brief recitation of his hopes for the school. "I didn't know how I'd make the school a reality until I found that brooch." He turned to Maggie and John. "The one that was so valuable by that French jeweler…" he hesitated.

"Van Cleef & Arpels," Maggie called out.

"Yep. That's the one. Maggie and John made everything possible by selling it and donating the proceeds to start Forever Guides."

"And Gordon Mortimer gave up his commission," Frank said, pointing to the tall man in the neat suit who had slipped in unobtrusively while David was speaking. "Plus an incredibly generous, anonymous donor matched the sales price," he finished.

Maggie looked at Gordon and held his gaze until he turned away.

"Thanks to these people, we have one million dollars to begin construction of the facilities we'll need to house a state-of-the-art guide dog training school."

The crowd erupted into applause.

Frank tapped the glass again. "Haynes Enterprises has acquired the vacant lot next door and will donate it for the Forever Guides campus."

Again, the room was filled with enthusiastic applause.

"Finally, I have one last announcement. I'm going to step away from the day-to-day operations of Haynes Operations to devote myself to Forever Guides and another program with Forever Friends that you'll learn more about in the coming days. Stepping in for me at Haynes Enterprises is Neil Parker." Frank motioned for Neil and Sherry to step forward.

"Please introduce yourselves and welcome Neil and his wife, Sherry—our new vet at Westbury Animal Hospital—to our community. I'm going to cut the cake. It's from Laura's, so you'll want to have a piece. Please stay and enjoy your-selves. The whole place is open, so feel free to look around. And if you find a furry friend that you'd like to take home with you, let me or David know. We'll get you all hooked up."

In the commotion, Maggie didn't hear her phone ring with the call from the chair of the board of the Highpointe College trustees. "Excuse me," she said to John and the Torreses. "I want to catch Gordon."

"You'd better hurry," Joan said. "It looks like he's headed for the door."

Maggie nodded and took off after him. She was convinced he was the anonymous matching donor. He might not want his identity known, but she needed to thank him. She wove her way through the crowd, oblivious to the ping that notified her of the lengthy voice mail message left by the trustee.

"Gordon," Maggie called as he strode to the parking lot.

He turned back to her, an uncharacteristic grin on his lips.

Maggie walked to him and threw her arms around his neck, giving him a tight hug.

He stood stiffly at first, then relaxed and hugged her back.

"You're a wonderful, kind, generous man, Gordon Mortimer," Maggie whispered in his ear. "I'm proud to know you." She released him in time to see the look of joy on his face.

THE END

THANK YOU FOR READING

If you enjoyed *When Dreams There Be*, I'd be grateful if you wrote a review.

Just a few lines on Amazon or Goodreads would be great. Reviews are the best gift an author can receive. They encourage us when they're good, help us improve our next book when they're not, and help other readers make informed choices when purchasing books. Goodreads reviews help readers find new books. Reviews on Amazon keep the Amazon algorithms humming and are the most helpful aide in selling books! Thank you.

To post a review on Amazon:

1. Go to the product detail page for *When Dreams There Be* on Amazon.com.

2. Click "Write a customer review" in the Customer Reviews section.

3. Write your review and click Submit.

In gratitude,
Barbara Hinske

JUST FOR YOU

Wonder what Maggie was thinking when the book ended? Exclusively for readers who finished *No Matter How Far*, take a look at Maggie's Diary Entry for that day at https://barbarahinske.com/maggies-diary.

ACKNOWLEDGMENTS

I'm blessed with the wisdom and support of many kind and generous people. I want to thank the most supportive and delightful group of champions an author could hope for:

My remarkable husband, Brian Willis, who never fails to steer me away from the rocks when ideas fail me;

My insightful and supportive assistant Lisa Coleman who keeps all the plates spinning;

My life coach Mat Boggs for your wisdom and guidance;

My kind and generous legal team, Kenneth Kleinberg, Esq., and Michael McCarthy—thank you for believing in my vision;

The professional "dream team" of my editors Linden Gross, Kelly Byrd, and proofreader Dana Lee;

Elizabeth Mackey for a beautiful cover.

RECURRING CHARACTERS

Recurring Characters

ACOSTA

Grace: older sister to Tommy; David Wheeler's high school sweetheart; plans to attend Highpointe College upon graduation; babysits for the Scanlons

Iris: mother to Grace and Tommy with husband, Kevin

Kevin: professor at Highpointe College

Tommy: became friends with Nicole Nash and David Wheeler while an in-patient at Mercy Hospital

Alistair: butler at Rosemont for over fifty years, now a friendly ghost who lives in the attic

John Allen: veterinarian and owner of Westbury Animal Hospital, Maggie Martin's husband, adopted grandfather to baby Julia and twins Sophie and Sarah

Anita Archer: owner of Archer's Bridal

Kevin Baxter: member of Highpointe College Board of Trustees

Marc Benson: partner of Alex Scanlon, musician

Nigel Blythe: owner of Blythe Rare Books in London, bought books stolen from Highpointe College Library, poisoned Hazel Harrington, attempted to kill Sunday Sloan and Anthony Plume

Harriet and Larry Burman: owners of Burman Jewelers

Jeff Carson: Widower; former wife, Millie, died 3 years ago; son Jason and daughter-in-law Sharon; grandchildren Tyler and Talia; cares about animal shelter; mother, Alma, uncle, William Olsson

Charlotte: owner of Candy Alley Candy Shop

DELGADO BROTHERS: involved in scheme to embezzle money from the Westbury Town Workers' Pension Fund

Chuck: former Westbury town councilmember; owner of D's Liquor and Convenience Store

Ron: investment advisor and CPA; married to William Wheeler's sister

FITZPATRICK

Laura: owner of Laura's Bakery; mother of one with husband, Pete

Pete: owner of Pete's Bistro, a popular lunch spot for Westbury town councilmembers

Gloria Harper: resident of Fairview Terraces, married to Glenn Vaughn, acts as surrogate grandmother to David Wheeler

Hazel Harrington: deceased rare-book librarian at Highpointe College, poisoned by Nigel Blythe

Robert Harris: rare-book librarian at Cambridge University, friend to Sunday Sloan

Frank Haynes: repentant crony of the Delgados, Westbury town councilmember, owner of Haynes Enterprises (holding company of fast food restaurants), founder and principal funder of Forever Friends dog rescue, grandson of Hector Martin, married to Loretta Nash, father of twins Bonnie and Branson

HOLMES

George: emcee of the annual Easter Carnival, father of three with wife, Tonya

Tonya: Westbury town councilmember; close friend of Maggie Martin

Russell Isaac: Westbury town councilmember, inherited auto parts business, former acting mayor of Westbury, involved in scheme to of Delgado brothers

Lyla Kershaw: works in accounting department at Highpointe College Library; close friend of Sunday Sloan; birth mother of Josh Newlon

Tim Knudsen: realtor, Westbury town councilmember, married to Nancy, grandfather to Zack

Ian Lawry: former president of Highpointe College

Ingrid: Haynes family nanny, former pediatric ICU nurse

Juan: veterinary technician at Westbury Animal Hospital

MARTIN

Amy: Maggie Martin's daughter-in-law; mother to twins, Sophie and Sarah, with husband, Mike Martin

Hector and Silas: deceased town patriarchs; Silas (Hector's father) amassed a fortune from the local sawmill, real estate, and other ventures and built the Rosemont estate; Hector donated his rare book collection to Highpointe College and left his estate to his living heirs—grandnephew, Paul Martin, and grandson, Frank Haynes (Frank's father was Hector's illegitimate son)

Maggie: current owner of Rosemont and president of Highpointe College; widow of Paul Martin; former forensic accountant and mayor of Westbury; married to John Allen; mother to Mike Martin and Susan (Martin) Scanlon; grandmother to Julia Scanlon and twins, Sophie and Sarah Martin

Mike: Maggie Martin's adult son, lives in California with wife, Amy, and twin daughters, Sophie and Sarah

Paul: Maggie Martin's first husband, deceased; embezzled funds while president of Windsor College; father of Susan (Martin) Scanlon and Mike Martin; had an affair with Loretta Nash and fathered Nicole Nash

Sophie and Sarah: twin daughters of Amy and Mike Martin; close friends of Marissa Nash; Maggie Martin's granddaughter

Mary: single mother who is the administrative assistant at Haynes Enterprises

Gordon Mortimer: antiques dealer and appraiser

NASH

Loretta: current financial analyst at Haynes Enterprises; married to Frank Haynes; mother to Marissa, Sean, and Nicole, with baby number four on the way; former mistress of Paul Martin

Marissa, Nicole, Sean: Loretta's children, adopted by stepfather, Frank Haynes; Marissa (oldest) babysits for the Scanlons and is friends with Maggie Martin's twin granddaughters; Nicole (youngest) received a kidney from Susan Scanlon after it was discovered that they had the same father, Paul Martin; Sean works as David Wheeler's apprentice at Forever Friends and the animal hospital

Bonnie and Branson: Frank and Loretta's twins

Josh Newlon: Maggie Martin's administrative assistant; Lyla Kershaw's birth son; Sunday Sloan's boyfriend

PARKER

Sherry and Neil: Sherry is the new veterinarian at Westbury Animal Hospital and her husband, Neil, is a graduate of The Warton School

Anthony Plume: professor and dean of English Literature at Highpointe College; stole rare books from the college library and sold them to Nigel Blythe

Jack Rodriguez: David Wheeler's landlord in California

SCANLON

Aaron: orthopedic surgeon; married to Maggie's daughter, Susan; father to baby Julia; brother to Alex

Alex: attorney who succeeds Maggie Martin as mayor of Westbury; partner of Marc Benson

Julia: infant daughter of Susan and Aaron Scanlon; Maggie Martin's granddaughter

Susan (née Martin): Maggie Martin's adult daughter; attorney works at brother-in-law Alex's firm; helped Josh Newlon find his birth mother; nearly died donating kidney to stepsister, Nicole Nash

Sunday Sloan: rare-book librarian at Highpointe College; friend of Lyla Kershaw; Josh Newlon's girlfriend

Forest Smith: attorney at Stetson & Graham; assigned to assist Alex Scanlon; died in a suspicious fall off a bridge

Bill Stetson: partner at Stetson & Graham, Westbury's outside law firm

Chief Andrew (Andy) Thomas: Westbury's chief of police

Joan and Sam Torres: wife and husband; Maggie Martin's close friends, who befriended her on her first day in Westbury; Joan works as a police dispatcher, Sam as a handyman

Lyndon Upton: professor of finance at University of Chicago, former colleague of Maggie Martin's; volunteered to help with Westbury's embezzlement case

Glenn Vaughn: resident of Fairview Terraces; married to Gloria Harper; acts as surrogate grandfather to David Wheeler

WHEELER

David: works with therapy dogs; helps at Forever Friends and Westbury Animal Hospital; son of William and Jackie Wheeler; Grace Acosta's boyfriend

Jackie: wife of disgraced former mayor William Wheeler; mother to David

William: former mayor of Westbury convicted for fraud and embezzlement; committed suicide in prison; father to David and husband to Jackie

Judy Young: business-savvy owner of Celebrations Gift Shop and town gossip; close friend of Maggie Martin; maiden name Jorgenson

RECURRING PETS

Westbury's Forever Friends

Blossom, Buttercup, and Bubbles—Maggie and John's kittens, named after PowerPuff Girls

Cooper—Susan and Aaron Scanlon's dog, a gift from David Wheeler. A young Golden Retriever who is calm and gentle with baby Julia

Daisy—Nash children's dog, an Aussie/cattle dog mix female

Dan—Josh Newlon's dog, huge black lab, has calming effect on baby Julia

Dodger—David Wheeler's dog, mid-sized mutt with one eye. Therapy dog

Dory—Jack Rodriguez's Westie

Eve—shows up at Rosemont on Maggie's first night, stray, small female terrier mix

Magellan—Tommy Acosta's cat

Namor—David Wheeler's cat whose name is Roman spelled backward, gray with 4 white paws

Roman—John Allen's dog, gentle Golden Retriever

Rusty—Sam and Joan Torres's dog

Sally—Frank Haynes' dog, overweight border collie mix

Snowball—Nash children's dog, a terrier/schnauzer mix male

Sparky—Tim Knudsen's grandson's dog/medium-sized crossbreed with curly brown and white coat

ABOUT THE AUTHOR

USA Today Bestselling Author BARBARA HINSKE is an attorney and novelist. She's authored the Guiding Emily series, the mystery thriller collection "Who's There?", the Paws & Pastries series, two novellas in The Wishing Tree series, and the beloved *Rosemont Series*. Her novella *The Christmas Club* was made into a Hallmark Channel movie of the same name in 2019.

She is extremely grateful to her readers! She inherited the writing gene from her father who wrote mysteries when he retired and told her a story every night of her childhood. She and her husband share their own Rosemont with two adorable and spoiled dogs. The old house keeps her husband busy with repair projects and her happily decorating, entertaining, and gardening. She also spends a lot of time baking and—as a result—dieting.

ENJOY THIS EXCERPT FROM
GUIDING EMILY

Prologue

Emily. The woman who would become everything to me. The person I would eat every meal with and lie down next to every night—for the rest of my days.

She was just ahead; behind that door at the far end of the long hall. I glanced over my shoulder. Mark kept pace, slightly behind me. I could feel his excitement. It matched my own.

Everyone said Emily and I would be perfect for each other. I'd overheard them talking when they thought I was asleep. I spend a lot of time with my eyes closed, but I don't sleep much. They didn't know that.

"A magical match," they'd all agreed.

I lifted my eyes to Mark, and he nodded his encouragement. I gave a brief shake of my head. Only four more doorways between Emily and me.

I picked up my pace. A cylindrical orange object on the carpet in the third doorway from the end caught my eye. *Is that a Cheeto? A Crunchy Cheeto? I love Crunchy Cheetos.*

I tore my eyes away.

This was no time to get distracted.

We sped across the remaining distance to the doorway at the end of the hall. The door that separated me from my destiny.

I froze and waited while Mark knocked.

I heard Emily's voice—the sound I would come to love above all others—say, "Come in."

What was that in her voice? Eagerness—anxiety—maybe even a touch of fear? I'd take care of all of that right away.

The door swung open and Mark stepped back. He pointed to Emily.

I'd seen her before. Emily Main was a beautiful young woman in her late twenties. Auburn hair cascaded around her shoulders and shone like a new penny. With my jet-black coloring, we'd make a striking couple.

"Go on," Mark said.

I abandoned all my training—all sense of decorum—and raced to her.

Emily reached for me and flung her arms around my neck.

I placed my nose against her throat, and she tumbled out of her chair onto her knees.

I swept my tongue over her cheek, tasting the saltiness of her tears.

"Oh … Garth." My name on her lips came out in a hoarse whisper.

I wagged my tail so hard that we both lay back on the floor. "Good boy, Garth!"

She rubbed the ridge of my skull behind my ears in a way that would become one of my favorite things in the whole wide world.

Next to food.

Especially Crunchy Cheetos.

Mark and the other trainers were right—we were made for each other. I was the perfect guide dog for Emily Main.

Chapter 1

"Weren't you supposed to leave for the airport half an hour ago?" Michael Ward asked his boss, whose fingers were typing furiously on her keyboard. "You're still planning to get married, aren't you?"

Emily Main's head bobbed behind the computer, her eyes fixed to the screen.

"I can't believe you put off a departure to Fiji to help us launch this new program. Your wedding's in two days."

"We've been working on this for almost a year. I wasn't about to leave when we're this close. I just need to finish this last email." She hunched forward and peered at the computer screen.

"There," she said, pushing her office chair back as the email *whooshed* from her inbox. "Done."

She looked up at Michael, blinking. It was probably the

first time she had looked at anything besides a computer screen in hours. "I brought my suitcase so I could go to the airport straight from the office. I don't have to stop at home."

Michael raised his eyebrows at her. "That's all you've got? A carry-on and a satchel for a week—a week that includes your wedding? My wife packs more than that for a three-day weekend."

"My wedding dress is a classic sheath and the rest is bathing suits and shorts."

"I would have thought Connor Harrington the third would have wanted an elaborate wedding—one fit for the society pages."

"Our wedding is going to be very elegant—think JFK Junior and Carolyn," Emily said, flinging her purse over her shoulder and reaching for the retractable handle of her suitcase.

Michael stepped in front of her. "I've got this," he said. "I'll walk you to the street. I'd like to congratulate Connor on snagging our office hero."

Emily hesitated.

"He is picking you up, isn't he? You're flying there together?"

"He went out over the weekend. He wanted to do some diving with his best man ... sort of a bachelor party reprise. I was traveling with my mom and maid of honor, but they flew out yesterday as planned. The company paid to change my ticket, but it would have cost almost five hundred dollars for Mom and Gina to change theirs. It wasn't worth it."

"But you don't like to fly." He peered into Emily's face.

"Did you talk to Connor about that before you decided to stay an extra day? You have told him about your fear of flying, haven't you?"

Emily shrugged. "I've mentioned it, sure, but I haven't made a big deal out of it."

"So what did he say?"

"He suggested that I get a prescription for Xanax and sleep the whole way out there."

"Really? That's what he said?"

"He's a Brit, for heaven's sake. 'Stiff upper lip' and all that. He's not the sort of guy to coddle anyone—and I'm not a needy type of gal. You know that."

Michael cocked his head to one side. "Do you have to change planes?"

Emily nodded.

"You don't want to be knocked out for that."

"I'll be fine." Emily threw her shoulders back. "You don't need to worry about me."

"I know—I'm sorry. It's just that I wouldn't let my wife make the trip alone if she felt like you do about flying."

"I fly alone all the time, and nothing's ever happened to me. There's no reason this time should be any different."

Michael lifted his hands, palms facing her, and shrugged. "Okay, but I think he could have at least offered to pay to change your mom's flight or something."

"I'll be perfectly fine." Emily walked past him into the hallway. "I promised Dhruv that I'd say goodbye before I leave."

"He's going to miss you. You're the one person here that really connects with him."

Michael watched her shoulders sag slightly.

"Hey," he said, rolling the carry-on to a halt beside her in the hall. "I'm sorry. I didn't mean to worry you. The whole team is going to step into your shoes while you're gone. We've talked about it."

"Of course you will. I shouldn't worry about him. I've got the best team in San Francisco. Scratch that. On the entire West Coast." Emily gave him a teary smile and punched him playfully on the shoulder. "I know you'll take care of everything while I'm away, Michael—including helping Dhruv stay connected with the team."

"Good!" Michael continued down the hallway. "I don't want you to give this place a second thought while you're gone. If anyone deserves a vacation—and a gorgeous beach wedding—it's you, Em. But don't get too comfortable." Michael turned and smiled at her. "We do need you to come back. We'd be lost without you here."

Emily laughed and pushed him toward the elevator. "Why don't you go push that button, you wonderful suck-up. It'll take ages to get an elevator this time of the morning. I'll stick my head into Dhruv's cubicle and be right back."

**

Emily found Dhruv, as usual, leaning into the bank of computer monitors, intently focused on the complex strings of code in front of him. She cleared her throat.

When Dhruv didn't move, she tapped him lightly on the shoulder.

Dhruv sat back quickly and spun around. A smile spread across his face when he saw her.

"I wanted to say goodbye before I go."

Dhruv nodded. "Goodbye."

"I'll see you a week from Monday."

"I know. You're getting married in two days, then you have your honeymoon for a week, then you come back to work," he recited.

"That's right. You remembered."

"I remember things."

"Yes, you do. That's one reason you're so very good at programming," she said.

"I know."

"Okay ... well ... have a good week. You can go to Michael if you have ... if you need anything."

"I know."

Emily regarded the shy, socially awkward middle-aged man who was, by far, the most proficient member of her extremely talented team of programmers. "Bye."

Dhruv nodded.

Emily stepped away.

Dhruv leapt out of his chair and called after her. "Have a happy wedding."

Emily swung around and gave him a thumbs-up then turned back toward the elevators where Michael was waiting.

From *Guiding Emily*

ALSO BY BARBARA HINSKE

Available at Amazon in Print, Audio, and for Kindle

The Rosemont Series

Coming to Rosemont

Weaving the Strands

Uncovering Secrets

Drawing Close

Bringing Them Home

Shelving Doubts

Restoring What Was Lost

No Matter How Far

When Dreams There Be

Novellas

The Night Train

The Christmas Club (adapted

for The Hallmark Channel, 2019)

Paws & Pastries

Sweets & Treats

Snowflakes, Cupcakes & Kittens (coming 2023)

Workout Wishes & Valentine Kisses

Wishes of Home

Novels in the Guiding Emily Series

Guiding Emily

The Unexpected Path

Over Every Hurdle

Down the Aisle

Novels in the "Who's There?!" Collection

Deadly Parcel

Final Circuit

CONNECT WITH BARBARA HINSKE ONLINE

Sign up for her newsletter at **BarbaraHinske.com**
Goodreads.com/BarbaraHinske
Facebook.com/BHinske
Instagram/barbarahinskeauthor
TikTok.com/BarbaraHinske
Pinterest.com/BarbaraHinske
Twitter.com/BarbaraHinske
Search for **Barbara Hinske on YouTube**
bhinske@gmail.com

Made in United States
Orlando, FL
20 April 2024

45987338R00193